BEWARE THE WEREPUP

AND OTHER STORIES

BEWARE THE WEREPUP

AND OTHER STORIES

4 BOOKS IN 1!

JULIE SYKES

ILLUSTRATED BY NATHAN REED

MACMILLAN CHILDREN'S BOOKS

Tiger Taming first published 2009 by Kingfisher
Dixie in Danger first published 2009 by Kingfisher
Parrot Pandemonium first published 2009 by Macmillan Children's Books
Beware the Werepup first published 2009 by Macmillan Children's Books

This bind-up edition published 2013 by Macmillan Children's Books
a division of Macmillan Publishers Limited
20 New Wharf Road, London N1 9RR
Basingstoke and Oxford
Associated companies throughout the world
www.panmacmillan.com

ISBN 978-1-4472-1961-3

1 3 5 7 9 8 6 4 2

A CIP catalogue record for this book is available from
the British Library.

Printed and bound by CPI Group (UK) Ltd, Croydon CR0 4YY

Contents

The Pet Sitter

TIGER TAMING

For Pat, Cara and Claire

CONTENTS

CHAPTER ONE
WANTED

Max ran all the way home from the shops even though it was the hottest day of the summer holidays so far. He arrived out of breath and with a trickle of sweat running down his nose.

'Mum,' he shouted, bursting through the back door, 'can I use the phone?'

'Max!' exclaimed Mum, looking up from the sink where she was peeling carrots. 'What's happened?'

Max stuck a skinny hand into the pocket of his trousers and eased out a scrap of paper. Carefully he laid it on the kitchen table. His heart was thumping loudly; partly because he'd run so fast in the heat and partly because he was scared Mum would say that he couldn't use the phone. He took a deep breath and forced himself to speak slowly and not gabble like he usually did when he was excited.

'Someone needs a pet sitter. There was an advert in the pet-shop window and I wrote it down. Listen to this.'

Max began to read from the slip of paper.

Mum laughed as she took the scrap of paper from Max and read the advert for herself. Max held his breath and willed her to say yes. He loved animals and was desperate for a pet, but he couldn't have one because of his big sister Alice. Alice was allergic to animals. They made her sneeze and gave her a rash.

'Well,' said Mum thoughtfully, 'it's a good idea, but if you take the job you'll have to see it through to the end. You can't give it up after a few days because you're bored with it.'

'As if!' exclaimed Max. 'I'd never get bored with it. You know how much I want a pet. I'll ring the number then, shall I?'

'Go on then.'

'Thanks, Mum,' said Max, hugging his mother.

Mum wanted to speak to Miss Itchy first so Max punched out her number on the keypad, then handed her the telephone. It rang six times before Miss Itchy answered and when Max heard her voice trill from the receiver his heart skipped a beat. Would the job still be available?

It was! Miss Itchy asked for Max to go round and meet her cat Tiger straight away. Max smoothed his unruly hair with his hands and put on his best, non-holed trainers. He was nervous and keen to make a good impression.

On the way round to Miss Itchy's house, Max tried to remember all the things he knew about cats. They were intelligent and independent creatures and they made good companions. Tiger was a good name, Max decided, imagining a huge stripy cat with tons of energy.

Max walked up and down Sea View Road several times before he found Miss Itchy's home, the Owl House. It was at the end of a narrow alley and Max walked past the entrance three times before he realized it was there! The alley ran between two high brick walls. It was a dark and creepy place and Max glanced nervously over his shoulder, sure that someone was following him. It was a relief when he reached the end of the alley and found a wooden gate with 'The Owl House' painted on it in wonky letters.

Max's hand trembled as he unlatched the gate and made his way along the path. He knew he would make an excellent pet sitter if only Miss Itchy would give him the chance to try. The door had an unusual bell; it was shaped like an owl with eyes that lit up when Max pushed it. It made no sound so Max pushed it again, but harder. This time the eyes flashed amber and from deep inside the house an owl hooted.

'Spooky!' said Max, half wanting to run away.

Suddenly the door opened, revealing a short dumpy lady dressed in black trousers and a gold shirt.

'Max?' she asked, and when Max nodded she smiled toothily and said, 'Come on in.'

Her creaky voice sent a shiver down Max's spine and he didn't move.

'Come along. No need to be shy.'

Miss Itchy wrapped her green fingernails around his arm and before, he could resist, Max was pulled inside the house.

CHAPTER TWO
PLAIN RIDICULOUS

Miss Itchy propelled Max along the hallway and into the kitchen, where black steam erupted from a huge pot boiling on the cooker.

'Ah good, the bat-wing juice is ready,' said Miss Itchy.

She lifted the lid and a bat flew out. Max jumped, but Miss Itchy ignored the bat. Spooning up some of the juice, she blew it cool, then sipped it noisily.

'Delicious! Want a taste?'

Max watched the bat escape through an open window and wished he could fly after it. Suddenly he wasn't sure that he wanted to be Miss Itchy's pet sitter. She was very strange and so was her curious house.

'No thanks,' he said, thinking he'd rather die of thirst than drink that stuff.

'Good-oh! All the more for me,' said Miss Itchy cheerfully. 'Right then. You've come about the pet-sitting job so I suppose you're going to ask me lots of questions.'

Max was surprised. He'd thought that Miss Itchy would want to ask *him* questions. Miss Itchy was the strangest person Max had ever met, but she was smiling in a kindly way so Max asked, 'When are you going away?'

'Right now. As soon as I've put the juice in the fridge. I make it up in bulk once a month.

Tiger loves bat-wing juice, but DON'T feed her any – it makes her do funny things.'

'What shall I feed her?' Max looked around the kitchen, hoping to catch a glimpse of Tiger, but there was no sign of the cat.

'Tiger eats tails. One tin a day, half in the morning and half at night, and a fishy biscuit if she's been good. She has two water bowls, one inside and one out. Everything you need is in the cupboard next to the fridge. Tiger can stay out all day, but bring her in at teatime and lock the cat flap. It's that easy! Any more questions?'

Max had two: why was Miss Itchy going away so quickly and was she, as he suspected, a witch? But the first question sounded nosey and the second plain ridiculous, so in the end he just said, 'Can I see Tiger?'

'Of course you can.'

Miss Itchy opened the back door and bellowed.

'Tiger, come here. You've got a visitor.'

It was a funny way to talk to an animal, but after a bit a lean black cat with one green eye and one blue strolled through the door. She gave Max a long, hard stare before settling

herself in a basket near the cooker to wash her ears. Max stared back, feeling disappointed. This plain, aloof creature was not how he had imagined Tiger to be. Miss Itchy turned to get her purse from a drawer and suddenly Tiger stuck her tongue out at Max.

Max stared. Had he imagined that? Tiger innocently continued her wash, but she was watching Max so he stuck his tongue out in return. Unfortunately Miss Itchy turned and caught him. Max reddened as Miss Itchy gave him a funny look.

'Still want the job?' she asked.

'Oh yes,' said Max. He had a weird feeling that Tiger

was laughing at him, but cats did not snigger or stick their tongues out at people, did they?

'Right then,' said Miss Itchy. 'I'll feed Tiger before I go so you can start tomorrow morning. This is the front-door key and here's your pay and I'll see you in one week.'

Max looked at the notes and coins Miss Itchy had shoved in his hand.

It seemed an awful lot of money for feeding her cat twice a day.

'Tiger's special,' said Miss Itchy, as if she could read his thoughts. 'There'll be BIG TROUBLE if anything happens to her while I'm away. I'm trusting you to take good care of her.'

A shiver tingled down Max's spine. There was no doubt that Miss Itchy meant every word she said. Well, he wouldn't disappoint her. Max would be Miss Itchy's best pet sitter ever. After all, he only had to feed Tiger twice a day. It couldn't be easier!

CHAPTER THREE
THREE BURGLARS

Early next morning Max let himself into the Owl House with the strange feather-shaped key Miss Itchy had given him. An owl hooted loudly when the front door swung open, causing Max to jump. Miss Itchy's house was full of surprises! Max followed the passage along to the kitchen and found it empty. There was no sign of Tiger, and her food from the night before was untouched in her bowl.

'Yikes!' Max exclaimed. It hadn't occurred to him that Tiger might not eat and he wasn't sure what to do next. Should he throw the food away and give her fresh food or did Miss Itchy make her eat the old stuff first?

But when Max looked at the bowl more closely he recoiled in horror. It was hardly surprising that Tiger hadn't eaten anything. The dish was full of tails. Rat tails,

mouse tails and something that might once have belonged to a cow.

'Gross!'

Max hunted around the kitchen until he found a spoon, then, letting himself out of the back door, he scraped the tails straight into the dustbin. The dish smelt foul and Max held it at arm's length to wash it clean in the enormous sink. He took a new tin of cat food from the cupboard, but when he opened it he found that it too was full of tails!

'Double gross!'

The writing on the tin read: *TAILS. Premium quality cat food. Squirrel and mouse variety.*

'If that's premium quality, I hate to think what economy's like,' said Max.

With his head turned to one side to avoid the smell, Max dished up half the tin and put it on the floor.

But where was Tiger? The cat flap was locked so she had to be in the house somewhere.

'Tiger?'

Max waited, but there was no padding of paws or friendly miaow.

'Tiger, where are you?'

Max listened and suddenly he became aware of voices. His heart beat faster. Who was it? Were there burglars in Miss Itchy's house? Max was suddenly scared. His first thought was to run, but he forced himself to stay calm. He hadn't found Tiger yet, and Miss Itchy had made it clear that there would be Big Trouble if anything happened to her cat while she was away.

Bravely Max crept in the direction of the voices. They were coming from behind a red door on the opposite side of the hall to the kitchen. Max stood with his hand on the doorknob. There was an argument going on inside; two girls were shouting at each other. They sounded like fighting hyenas and reminded Max of his sister Alice when she was in one of her strops.

Max listened, then suddenly he laughed. He recognized those voices now as belonging to two characters in a TV soap. Miss Itchy must have forgotten to turn the television off before she left. Still laughing, Max opened the door, then gasped at the sight before him.

Tiger was sprawled on the sofa surrounded by a pile of fishy biscuits and several empty crisp bags. A can of fizzy lime, sprouting a long bendy straw, was propped up against the cushions beside her. The television was on with the sound at full blast and Max quickly reached for the remote control to turn the volume down.

Tiger twisted her head round and glared at Max.

'Turn it up. I'm watching this.'

'Pardon?'

For a second Max thought that it was Tiger who'd spoken, but, realizing how ridiculous that was, he glanced around to see who else was there. The room was empty.

'Turn it up, birdbrain!'

'No, I won't, dogbreath!' Max retorted, then suddenly realizing he was arguing with a cat he added, 'You can talk?'

'So? Don't tell me you've never heard a cat talk before.'

'No!' said Max excitedly, 'I haven't.'

'Fish-for-brains! Turn the TV up and go away.'

'Fish-for-brains yourself. I'm Max, your pet sitter. Remember me now? I'm looking after you this week.'

'Pet sitter! Ha! That's a joke! I don't need a boy to look after me.'

Max's excitement at finding a talking cat fizzled away like a spent firework. He had always wanted to be able to communicate with animals – just his luck to get a stroppy one!

'Look,' he said firmly, 'Miss Itchy asked me to look after you, and I promised her I would. I've put your breakfast in the kitchen, so off you trot like a good little pussycat and eat it while I clear up this mess.'

Tiger stood up and stretched. In two nimble jumps she went from the back of the sofa to the top of a tall pine dresser, from where she stared defiantly down at Max.

'Make me,' she said.

CHAPTER FOUR
BAT-WING JUICE

Max was furious but he fought back his rising temper.

'Come down,' he said. 'It's dangerous up there.'

'Fish-face!' said Tiger, rudely sticking her tongue out.

Max glanced at his watch. He'd been longer than he thought, and if he didn't go home soon, Mum would worry. It was tempting to leave Tiger where she was, but suppose she fell and hurt herself? Miss Itchy would blame him and Max did not want to get on her wrong side! There was only one thing for it. If Tiger wouldn't come down then he, Max, would have to climb up and get her.

There was a straight-backed chair in the corner of the room. Max thought he might be able to reach Tiger if he stood on it. He moved the chair in front of the dresser, but as he straightened up something hit him on the shoulder.

'Ow!'

Max winced and stared at the book that moments before had been propped on the dresser.

Tiger smirked. 'There's more where that came from.'

So far as Max could see, there were no more books on the dresser, but there were plenty of other items that Tiger could throw at him – all of them breakable.

'I'll come down if there's bat-wing juice for breakfast.'

'No deal,' said Max, remembering Miss Itchy had warned him not to feed Tiger bat-wing juice.

'Why not?' demanded Tiger. 'Oh, don't tell me! Warble Itchy wants the bat-wing juice all for herself. Greedy pig!'

'You're not allowed bat-wing juice. It makes you do funny things.'

'I can do funny things without drinking juice,' said Tiger. 'Watch this.'

Daintily she flicked her tail and knocked a framed photograph of Miss Itchy off the dresser. The photo fell face down and splinters of glass pinged across the wooden floor.

Tiger laughed raucously. Then, swishing her tail, she edged closer to a dainty china cauldron.

'Wait!' said Max.

Tiger narrowed her eyes, then lined her tail up with the cauldron. 'This cauldron's special. It cost a fortune.'

That did it! Max knew he'd have to get the photograph frame fixed before Miss Itchy returned from her holiday. He couldn't risk having to buy an expensive china cauldron too. Surely a tiny drink of juice couldn't make Tiger any worse than she already was?

'OK,' he said, holding up his hands in defeat. 'Come down and I'll get you some bat-wing juice.'

CHAPTER FIVE
THE PARTY

Tiger drank daintily, then Max let her out into the garden, where she curled up under a bush to snooze in the morning sun. She seemed more friendly now she'd had some bat-wing juice and Max decided that she might be right about Miss Itchy being greedy.

'I'll be back at teatime,' said Max.

'Don't rush,' said Tiger lazily. 'I'd rather be outside than locked indoors. There's more to do out here.'

Max agreed with that. It was the summer holidays and he'd planned to spend the day on the beach with his best friend, Joe. He couldn't wait to tell Joe about Tiger, only he thought he'd leave the talking bit out. Joe would think that was mad. After all, Max could hardly believe it himself! Max was looking forward to seeing Tiger again.

Straight after tea Max hurried along Sea View Road towards the spooky alley that led to the Owl House.

The little tabby cat that lived in one of the houses next to the alley was sitting on the wall and howled loudly as Max passed by. Max felt the hair at the back of his neck stand up! What could have made the cat cry out like that?

Then Max turned into the alley and heard a terrible screeching reply. Immediately he broke into a run. He had a bad feeling about that noise. It sounded like the tabby was talking to another cat. Max hoped Tiger was all right.

By the time Max reached Miss Itchy's gate he was panting and he had a stitch. He stood for a second to get his breath back. Then, as he opened the gate, he was blasted with ice-cold water.

'Yeow! What the . . .' spluttered Max.

'Bullseye!' screamed a familiar voice and there were howls of laughter.

'TIGER!'

Crossly Max pushed his dripping fringe  off his face and wiped the water from his eyes.

'What was that for?'

'Getting our own back.' The tabby appeared from behind Max and stared nastily at him. 'Now you know how it feels when we're having a singsong at night and someone throws a bucket of water at us.'

'Not me!' said Max indignantly. 'I've never done that.'

'Your dad did
last week,' said
a ginger cat,
appearing out
of the bushes
and standing
next to the tabby.
'We were right in the middle of verse two
when your dad opened an upstairs window
and threw water over us.'

'Oh well, that makes it all right then,'
said Max sarcastically. 'Are you happy
now?'

No one bothered to answer so Max said
crossly, 'It's teatime, Tiger. You'd better say
goodbye to your friends now and come
inside.'

'No way!' said Tiger. 'We're having a
party. It's Red Eye's eightieth.'

Suddenly cats of all shapes and sizes came out of the bushes and squeezed next to each other on the overgrown path. They didn't look too friendly, and Max took a nervous step backwards. A small grey cat with bright red eyes chuckled, then, holding a bottle to his lips, he took a swig of the contents before passing it on to Tiger.

'What's that you're drinking?' asked Max suspiciously.

'Bat-wing juice.' Tiger smacked her lips noisily. 'Red Eye's witch makes it a lot stronger than Warble Itchy does. It's delicious. Want some?'

'No way! And you've had enough too,' said Max. 'Come along, Tiger. It's time to go in.'

There was a horrible noise like rusty hinges creaking in the wind as the cats doubled up with laughter.

'Come along, Tiger,' they mimicked. 'Time to go in and have your tea like a good little pussycat.'

Tiger laughed with them and stayed where she was, one paw firmly grasping the bottle of bat-wing juice.

It was hopeless! Max couldn't leave Tiger out all night but he didn't have a clue how to get her indoors. Miss Itchy had been right. The juice was definitely having a funny effect. Tiger was swaying slightly and she kept shrieking with laughter for no reason. Max decided his best plan was to make a sudden grab for the cat and carry her indoors. He turned his back on her to make her think he was going home, but before he could grab her Max heard the clatter of claws coming along the alley.

'More trouble!' he groaned, and he was right.

Two powerful dogs were rushing towards the Owl House at such speed Max doubted they would stop. Their enormous bodies took up the whole of the alley with no room to spare so they looked like a monstrous,

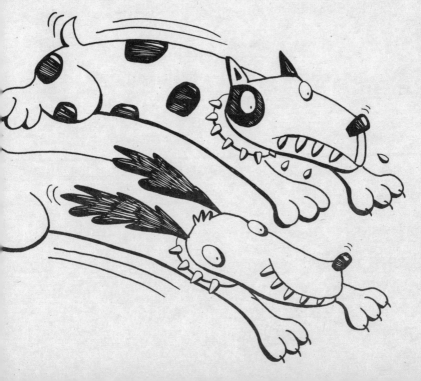

two-headed, eight-legged beast. Max felt his insides melt.

'Run!' he yelled, and he fled towards the Owl House.

CHAPTER SIX
THE GATECRASHERS

Max pushed the key into the lock and forced open the front door. Tiger shot in ahead of him and, in spite of his own fear, the sight of her with her fur fuzzed out like a loo brush made Max laugh.

Tiger fled upstairs, and from somewhere in the house an owl let out a blood-curdling screech. Max slammed the front door shut and bolted it for extra safety. Then he ran to the cat flap and locked that too. When he looked out of the window all the cats in Miss Itchy's garden had disappeared. Only the two dogs were visible. Glued

shoulder to shoulder, they prowled slowly around the garden, growling and sniffing at everything.

'Tiger,' called Max, 'where did all your mates go?' There was no reply. Max climbed the stairs and looked around, but Tiger had hidden well and he couldn't find her. Sighing, Max went to the kitchen to dish up her tea. He found the bowl of tails from breakfast untouched. Max didn't dare go outside to put it in the dustbin so he spooned out the rest of the tin on top. He doubted that Tiger would eat it anyway.

Max wondered who the dogs belonged to. He knew most of the local dogs, but he definitely hadn't seen these ones before and they weren't the sort you forgot in a hurry. Max watched out of the window, expecting their owner to come and claim them. But no one appeared and after a long while the dogs left the garden and slunk, side by side, back down the alley. It was getting late, but Max waited another ten minutes to make sure the dogs had gone for good. He didn't fancy meeting them on his way home.

'Bye, Tiger.'

No answer.

'See you in the morning,' Max shouted up the stairs.

As Max let himself out of the Owl House an owl hooted goodbye. Max

47

grinned, thinking the unusual doorbell could teach Tiger a thing or two about manners. At home Max collapsed on his bed. One day over, but six more to go. It seemed an awfully long time to be a pet sitter.

CHAPTER SEVEN
CATNAPPED

The following morning Max vowed he would be firmer with Tiger. He wouldn't let her bully him into feeding her bat-wing juice, and if she started throwing things then he'd threaten to bring the dogs back. Max felt much happier – until he reached the Owl House. He could hear the owl hooting even as he came along the alley. It was going non-stop like a burglar alarm. *Hoo, Hoo, Hoo, Hoo, Hoo!*

With a sinking feeling Max let himself into the house. This had to be something to do with Tiger but whatever was she up to now?

'Tiger!'

Max yelled to make himself heard above the din. 'Tiger, what's going on?'

When there was no answer Max checked the lounge, but this morning the television was off and the room was tidy. The kitchen was empty too and, Max noticed in surprise, so was Tiger's food bowl.

'Poo!' he said, prodding the dish with his toe.

The empty dish reeked and the bowl of water next to it was full of slobber. Max stared at it thoughtfully. Cats didn't slobber, but dogs did and a nasty suspicion crossed Max's mind.

Quickly Max searched the remaining downstairs rooms, then mounted the stairs. The owl doorbell was still hooting and as Max climbed the staircase the noise grew louder. It sounded so lifelike that Max wondered whether he should be looking for an owl as well as for Tiger.

'Tiger?' he called. 'Where are you?'

Max searched every room thoroughly, but they were all empty. There was no sign of Tiger and definitely no owl. Now Max's heart began to pound like running feet. How could Tiger have disappeared? He went back to the kitchen and checked the cat flap. It was locked, just as he'd known it would be. Max clearly remembered locking it after the fierce dogs had chased him into the house.

Unsure what to do next Max went back to the hall and collided with Red Eye, who had run in through the open front door.

'Thank goodness you're here,' panted the little grey cat. 'Tiger's in trouble. You've got to save her.'

'Save her from what?' asked Max, wondering if this was another practical joke.

'Grimboots,' said Red Eye.

'Grimboots who?'

'GRIMBOOTS!' shouted Red Eye, and Max saw he was trembling. 'You must have heard of Grimboots. He's the meanest wizard in the world. His dogs took Tiger away last night and they said Grimboots is going to turn her into a pair of gloves.'

'Ah, *that* Grimboots!' said Max, deciding this was a joke. 'So how did his dogs get in when all the doors were locked?'

'Magic, of course,' said Red Eye impatiently. 'Can't you hear the sneak alarm going? I'd better turn him off.'

Red Eye leaped up the stairs and opened a small door that Max had thought was a cupboard. The door led into the eaves of the house.

'It's all right, Otus,' called Red Eye. 'Help's arrived. The boy's here.'

Immediately the hooting stopped, and as

Red Eye pulled the door shut Max heard the rustle of wings and caught a glimpse of a large amber eye.

'Oh!' he exclaimed, pleased that the owl was real.

'Go on,' said Red Eye, suddenly brisk. 'Off you go and rescue Tiger.'

'Right,' said Max. 'Silly me! Er . . . so how would I do that then?'

'Go to Seaweed Island and bring her back,' said Red Eye.

'And where is Seaweed Island?'

Red Eye hissed angrily. 'Don't you know Seaweed Island? It's in the middle of the ocean. Grimboots lives there with his dogs.'

'You want me to go to Seaweed Island?' said Max. 'On my own?'

'You're the pet sitter,' said Red Eye. 'I can't go. I hate water and I hate dogs! Besides, this has nothing to do with me. It's Warble's fault. She sold Grimboots a potion to stop his hair from going white, but it didn't work and it made ALL his hair fall out instead. Grimboots is balder than a baby. No hair anywhere, not even up his nose.'

'Couldn't he magic it back again?' asked Max.

'The spell was too powerful,' said Red Eye. 'Warble's gone to see her old teacher to see if she can help to put things right, but Grimboots is so angry he wants revenge. He vowed to get his own back on Warble Itchy and now he has. Tiger is Warble's best friend.'

'And you want me to row over to Seaweed Island and ask Grimboots to give Tiger back?' asked Max incredulously. 'Some chance! His dogs would eat me first!'

'It's too far to row. You'll have to fly,' said Red Eye. 'Luckily Warble left her broom behind. She's too fat to ride it. Off you go then.'

Max's heart began to pound.

'Go now, in the daylight? Won't Grimboots see me coming?'

'Grimboots doesn't go out in the daylight

since he lost his hair. He's gone nocturnal. It's just the dogs you have to worry about. Warble's broom has an invisibility switch so you can fly without being seen. Keep upwind from them so they don't smell you and you'll be fine.'

Max gulped. It sounded simple, but those dogs were vicious. One snap of their enormous jaws and he, Max Barker, would be history. Max was very tempted to run home for his pet-sitting money – he hadn't spent any of it yet. He would give the money back and quit the job. But he remembered what his mum had said and knew it didn't work like that. Once he'd agreed to look after Tiger, the cat was his responsibility until Miss Itchy returned home.

'I can't fly,' he said feebly.

'I'll teach you. It's really easy,' said Red Eye persuasively. 'Warble's broom is in the second room on the right. Go and get it and bring it to the garden.'

The broom was propped against the wall next to a rack of wands. Max sized the wands up, then unhooked the biggest one. It was too long to fit in his pocket but there was a clip on the underside of the broom that made an excellent wand–holder. Max fixed the wand in place, then carried the broom outside.

CHAPTER NINE
FLYING

'**K**eep still,' bawled Red Eye. 'You're riding a broomstick, not a bicycle.'

Max stopped pedalling his legs and immediately fell forward.

'Sit up!' Red Eye yelled.

Max tried, but it was really hard to sit straight without feeling like he was going to topple off.

'Sit up!' shouted Red Eye again as the broom lurched into a dive.

Max sat up too quickly. The broom wobbled and he fell off, landing in Miss Itchy's compost heap.

'Yuck!'

Max picked a slug out of his hair and a banana skin from his shoe.

'You've nearly got it,' said Red Eye kindly. 'Let's try again.'

Max had been trying for ages and he didn't feel like he'd nearly got it at all. He was covered in bruises and his bottom hurt

from sitting on the hard broom handle. It was hopeless. He was never going to be good enough to fly to Seaweed Island, let alone rescue Tiger and fly back with her. He might as well face it. He, Max Barker, was in Big Trouble. When Miss Itchy returned and found Tiger was missing, she would probably turn *Max* into a pair of gloves!

But Max didn't give up. Six attempts later he flew a triumphant loop the loop in Miss Itchy's garden. With Red Eye's help he'd done it – he'd finally learned to ride a broomstick! Now all Max had to do was fly to Seaweed Island and rescue Tiger. It sounded easy, but the thought of Grimboots and his dogs made Max feel quite queasy.

'Well done!' said Red Eye, thumping his tail on the ground. 'I'd say you were ready to go.'

'I don't know how to get there,' said Max.

'That's the easy bit,' said Red Eye. 'Tell the broom where you want to go and it'll fly you straight there.'

Max took a deep breath. This was it then. No more excuses. He climbed astride the broom, flicked the invisibility switch on and waved a goodbye to Red Eye. The little grey cat ignored him.

'Bye,' called Max.

Red Eye jumped.

'Don't do that! I thought you'd gone,' he said.

Max chuckled and felt braver now he knew the invisibility switch worked.

'Broom, take me to Seaweed Island,' he commanded.

At first the broom shuddered as if it didn't want to go to Seaweed Island but slowly it rose in the air and flew towards the sea.

It was a sunny day and the beaches were crowded with holidaymakers. Max wondered what would happen if he fell off and became visible again. That would take some explaining!

Seaweed Island was miles away. Max wondered how Grimboots and his two dogs travelled there. Did they fly by broomstick or did they go by boat? Max saw several boats but as he neared Seaweed Island the sea mysteriously emptied.

Remembering what Red Eye had said, Max asked the broom to land upwind of the dogs. The two creatures lived in kennels outside Grimboots's tall stone tower. Max heard them snarling as he flew over the island and prepared to land in a small copse of trees. It was a bumpy landing and Max hoped the dogs hadn't heard him.

He unclipped Warble's wand, then, making the broom visible so he could find it again, he hid the broom under a bush. That was the easy part of the plan and Max was dreading the next bit. Feeling like a burglar, he nervously crept across the island. Even though his feet made no sound, he was sure the noise of his thudding heart would give him away! Several agonizing minutes later Max reached the tower, and there his simple plan to rescue Tiger came unstuck. The tower had no windows or doors. So far as Max could see, there was no way of getting inside!

'Hmmm,' said Max thoughtfully.

Silently he crept around the tower, but he found nothing. There wasn't so much as a crack in the rough stone walls. There had to be a way in, but where? Suddenly the answer came to Max; if there weren't any doors, there had to be a secret tunnel. Max retraced his steps and on his third time round the tower he found what he was looking for – a wooden door almost hidden in the sandy earth. The door had no handle and Max

couldn't see a way of opening it until Miss Itchy's wand began to twitch violently.

'Of course!' Max exclaimed, and he pointed the twitching wand at the door.

ZAP!

A jet of gold stars shot from the wand and the door opened.

'Thanks, wand,' whispered Max.

It was dark inside the tower but Max could see two sets of stairs, one spiralling upwards, the other down. He paused, wondering which way to go. He guessed that one of those staircases would lead him to Tiger and the other to the sleeping Grimboots, but which one was which? It was the wand that came to his aid again. It twitched violently, then sent a river of silver stars over the downward staircase.

'Thanks,' whispered Max, and feeling braver because of the wand, he started down the stairs.

CHAPTER TEN
THE RESCUE

Max ran his hand along the rough stone wall as he tiptoed down the staircase. He always got butterflies when he was nervous, but right now his stomach was fluttering like it was full of bats! It was a long way down, but finally Max reached the bottom. A steel door barred his way. Frustrated, Max banged on it, then jumped as something on the other side squealed.

Recovering himself, Max examined the door. There was a small square flap cut into the bottom. Max crouched down and saw the flap was secured with a single bolt.

Wondering what he would find, Max slid the bolt back, then pushed at the flap. It opened inwards and Max held it up with one hand while he peered through it. A cold, damp smell wafted out and Max wrinkled his nose in disgust. His eyes searched the gloom and after a bit he made out a shadowy form huddled in the corner.

'Tiger?' he whispered.

'Max!'

The shadow grew like a balloon, then split apart into three shapes. Cats. Two stayed where they were but the skinny black cat with odd coloured eyes came to the door to stare accusingly at Max.

'What kept you?' hissed Tiger crossly. 'You've been ages.'

'Charming,' said Max. 'I'll go away if you're going to be grumpy.'

'No, wait,' said Tiger. 'I didn't mean it. Please get me out of here.'

Max grinned to himself. It was the first time he'd heard Tiger say please.

The other cats came over and pushed their noses through the flap.

'Will you rescue us too?' they asked.

'Yes,' said Max. 'Stand back. We don't have much time.'

Max was beginning to enjoy the power of Miss Itchy's wand. He waved it around, then rapped it smartly on the door. There was a loud crack and a jet of red flame blasted the hinges skywards. The door groaned then fell inwards, almost squashing Tiger and her cellmates.

'Wicked!' exclaimed Max.

'Careful!' snapped Tiger, picking her way through the wreckage. 'That's Warble's most powerful wand!'

The two other cats ran out of their prison cell and wrapped themselves around Max's legs.

'Thank you for saving us,' miaowed the cat with the white paws. 'I'm Left and this is my brother, Right. Grimboots

was going to turn us into earmuffs.'

The more Max heard about Grimboots, the less he wanted to meet him. Quickly he led everyone back up the stairs and out through the trapdoor in the ground. The three cats blinked and sneezed in the sunlight and Max gave them a few seconds to get used to the brightness before moving on.

It was a relief to leave Grimboots's sinister tower behind, and Max gave a silent cheer when they finally reached the copse of trees where he'd hidden the broom.

'We did it!' he whispered triumphantly. 'We're free!'

But Max had spoken too soon. To his horror, when he crawled under the bush to retrieve the hidden broom, he found nothing.

'You probably hid it somewhere else,' said Tiger.

'I didn't!' Max insisted.

Suddenly Tiger went rigid. Her fur stood out like porcupine quills. Then, hissing like a steam train, she launched herself into the nearest tree. Left and Right followed.

Behind him Max heard the scrabble of claws and a fearful snarling.

'Hide!' shrieked Tiger from up in the tree.

Max put one hand on the tree trunk, but before he could climb up, Grimboots's

two thuggish
dogs crashed
into the clearing.

'Lost something?'
snarled one.

The other dog growled and Max
gasped, for clamped between the
beast's jaws was the missing broom.

At that moment Max's courage
failed. Helplessly he watched the
snarling dogs come closer.

Move, thought Max. Move
now or you'll end up as dog

food. But still his legs wouldn't work. Then he remembered his wand. Max pointed it at the biggest dog.

ZAP!

A jet of orange flame shot towards the dog, who leaped up and swallowed it with one greedy gulp. The dog lunged at Max and snatched the wand from his hand.

Neat trick! thought Max, despite his terror, for what chance did he have now, with no wand to defend himself?

CHAPTER ELEVEN
FIGHTING GRIMBOOTS

'**M**ax!' shouted Tiger.

Max turned and his heart leaped. Tiger was leaning out of the tree with a paw outstretched to help Max to safety.

'Max, quick.'

Max stretched up the tall tree trunk towards Tiger's paw, but he couldn't quite reach it.

'STOP!'

It was a voice not to be argued with and Max froze. A stocky wizard with a billowing cape and tall purple hat strode through the trees.

'So, you're Warble's new apprentice, are you? Not for long!' said the wizard nastily, aiming his wand at Max. 'You'll make a tasty supper for my dogs.'

Max was confused. Who was this? It couldn't be Grimboots, as this wizard had a

fine head of hair. Max could see it sticking out from under his hat in great fuzzy clumps.

Suddenly Max heard something snap. Then a large branch flew out of the tree towards the wizard.

'Run,' shouted Tiger, throwing a second branch.

Max couldn't run. He just stared. Tiger's shot had knocked off the wizard's hat, revealing a bald head shinning in the morning sun. It was Grimboots. The hair was a wig! The wig landed on one of the dog's backs, and the other dog sniffed it suspiciously. In spite of the danger, Max couldn't help himself. He roared with laughter!

'Silence!' shouted Grimboots. 'It's not funny. No one laughs at me.'

Max tried to stop laughing, but he couldn't. It was always like this when he was nervous. Once something started him off, he just couldn't stop; laughing at the wrong thing had got him into trouble heaps of times at school.

'Dogs, get him!'

The dogs ignored Grimboots. They sniffed curiously at the hairy wig, pawing it with their large feet.

Max heard a rustle above his head, then, in a surprise attack, Tiger launched herself at Grimboots. She landed on his back and was joined by Left and Right. Grimboots howled with rage and his dogs flew at the cats. Tiger scrambled on to Grimboots's head and wrapped her paws around his eyes. Grimboots tried to pull her off, but Left grabbed one of his arms and Right grabbed the other and together they pinned them to his sides. Grimboots shook his head furiously and Tiger started slipping.

'Hang on, Tiger,' yelled Max.

He was about to join the fight when he noticed Warble's wand and broom abandoned on the ground. A better idea came to him and he seized them both.

'Broom, up,' he commanded, standing astride it.

The broom rose and Max slid sideways.

He clung on, stopped pedalling his legs, sat up straight and then he was flying properly. The air beneath him was thick with grunts and squawks. Max flew in a circle above the fight while he planned his next move. Then, flicking the broom's invisibility switch on, he whispered, 'Broom, dive.'

The broom obeyed and Max felt he'd left his stomach behind as he sped earthwards. A few centimetres from Grimboots's shiny bald head, Max reached out, grabbed Tiger by the scruff of her neck and zoomed away. Tiger struggled and spat and Max wasted precious seconds convincing her that she was being rescued!

Confident of success, Max dived twice more, snatching first a surprised Left and then Right from Grimboots's arms. The broom dipped with the extra weight and

Max urged it higher. Seconds later Grimboots realized he was fighting his own dogs.

'Fools!' he bellowed angrily.

The dogs caught the scent of the escaping party and jumped and snapped at the empty air. Max flew higher, still skilfully dodging the blue flames shooting from Grimboots's wand.

'HOME!' he commanded and the broom banked sharply.

Minutes later Seaweed Island was a shrinking dot in the middle of the sea.

'We did it!' cried Max triumphantly.

CHAPTER TWELVE
MISS ITCHY RETURNS

'You came back then,' said Tiger, as Miss Itchy dumped her suitcase in the hall.

'Hello, Max,' said Miss Itchy.

She ignored her cat and went straight to the kitchen, where she poured herself a large mug of bat-wing juice.

'You came back then,' Tiger repeated, jumping up on the table.

'Juice, Max? No? Good-oh! More for me,' said Miss Itchy, taking a long drink. At last she put the mug down and, wiping her mouth with her sleeve, she asked, 'Why? Did you think I'd gone for good?'

'Didn't know what to think when you scuttled off like that,' said Tiger sulkily. 'You usually take me with you.'

Max was amazed. Suddenly he realized why Tiger had been so awful when he'd first started this pet-sitting job. She hadn't wanted to stay at home.

'Grimboots was after me,' said Miss Itchy. 'Home was the safest place for you.'

'Clearly not,' said Tiger.

Tiger told Miss Itchy what had happened while she'd been away. She was cross with her owner. 'You put Max in a lot of danger,' she said.

'He loved it, didn't you, Max?' Miss Itchy poked Max with a long green nail.

Max grinned and his eyes sparkled as he remembered the adventures of the last week. He'd been more scared than he cared to remember, but Miss Itchy was right. He'd *loved* the excitement and, best of all, he'd made a new friend. Tiger.

'See!' said Miss Itchy triumphantly. 'Max is the *best* pet sitter ever. You'd pet-sit again, wouldn't you, Max?'

'Yes,' said Max, glowing with pride.

'Did you find out how to undo the spell?' Tiger asked grumpily. 'Will Grimboots get his hair back?'

'I know how to fix it, but I've a good mind to

leave him bald after the trouble he's caused,' said Miss Itchy.

'No way!' squawked Tiger. 'Max might not be here for me next time. Give Grimboots the potion.'

Miss Itchy banged her mug on the table.

'All right,' she muttered. 'If I have to. And what about you, Max? Can I give your telephone number to my friends? Pet sitters are hard to find these days, and a good one like you is as rare as Grimboots being nice.'

Max beamed at Miss Itchy. Not only had she called him the best pet sitter ever, but she was offering to get him more pet-sitting work. He could hardly wait to get started!

'Yes, please,' he agreed. 'Max the Pet Sitter is waiting for that call!'

Me and Tiger

The Pet Sitter

DiXiE iN DANGER

For Alistair, Will, Tim and Antonia

CONTENTS

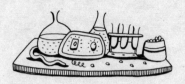

Chapter One
An Emergency

Max raced in from the garden and through the back door, where he snatched at the ringing phone.

'Max?' said an impatient voice. 'Max, the pet sitter?'

'Yes,' said Max.

Max had been pet-sitting for a while now and had looked after some unusual animals for some very strange owners.

'This is an emergency,' the voice continued. 'I have to go away right now and I need someone to take care of my pet dormouse. Her name's Dixie. Can you do it?'

'Sure,' said Max, checking his watch. He was looking after a troupe of zebra fish and they were due a dancing lesson at three thirty, but there was plenty of time to go and meet Dixie first. 'What's your name and where do you live?'

'I'm Ivor, Ivor Gadget, and I live at 36 Sandy Road. Look, this really is an emergency. Can you come straight away?'

'Already left!' said Max cheerfully, hanging up.

Max went upstairs to get his pet sitter's notebook. This was a small hardback book with a picture of a whale on the cover. In it

Max wrote down the names of the animals he was pet-sitting and notes on their care. Max kept his notebook buried in his sock drawer. It was a simple but safe hiding place. Alice, his bossy big sister, was always nosing into his business. But she wouldn't dream of touching his socks, not for anything!

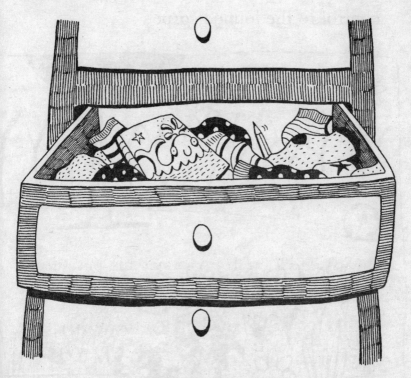

Max shoved the notebook and a pencil in his pocket, then ran downstairs to the garden. Alice had gone outside to practise her dance moves; her legs were everywhere and her bottom stuck up in the air. Max couldn't help himself. It was time to get Alice back for telling on him yesterday when he accidently glued the TV remote control to the lounge carpet.

Max gave her bottom a small shove, then legged it as Alice toppled head first into the snapdragons.

'Max!' she shrieked. 'I'll get you for that!'

'You'll have to catch me first,' said Max, running into the garden shed. He was on his bike and cycling up the garden before Alice was back on her feet.

'Whatever is going on?' asked Mum,

coming out of the back door. 'Why is Alice sitting in the flowers?'

'Perhaps she thinks they'll make her smell nicer,' chuckled Max. 'I'm going out. I've got another job.'

'Not so fast, young man. Where and who?'

'Aw, Mum!' Max stopped a safe distance

from Alice, who was mouthing threats at him. 'Sandy Road, number 36. Ivor Gadget wants me to look after his dormouse.'

'A dormouse!' exclaimed Mum. 'I've never heard of keeping a pet dormouse. Oh well, have fun and be back by teatime.'

'I will,' said Max. 'Thanks, Mum. Bye, Alice.'

He waved at his sister. It felt good to get the better of her for a change!

Sandy Road wasn't far, and as Max pedalled along he tried to imagine what sort of person kept a dormouse. They weren't exactly challenging animals. From what Max could remember, dormice were nocturnal and spent up to three-quarters of their life asleep.

'I bet Ivor Gadget is ancient,' Max panted. 'That's why he's got a dormouse.

He'll be an old man with grey hair and wrinkles.'

Max turned the corner of Sandy Road and looked at the house numbers. The evens were on his left-hand side and he counted them off.

'30 . . . 32 . . . 34 . . . there it is!'

Number 36 was slightly different from the other houses. Instead of having a small brick wall, the front garden was surrounded by a high fence. Max parked his bike and looked for a gate, but there wasn't one. The fence stretched in an unbroken line the whole way around the house. So how did he get in? Carefully Max studied the fence. It was very high, but he was good at climbing. Max thought if he stood on the next-door neighbour's brick wall he could easily climb over. Max spat on his hands, then wiped

them down his shorts to
give himself better grip.
He scrambled on to the
brick wall, but as he
reached up to the fence he
heard a sharp click followed by
a whirring noise. Looking up, Max

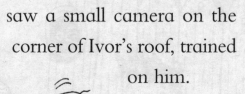

saw a small camera on the
corner of Ivor's roof, trained
on him.

'Name?'
asked a metallic
voice.

Suspiciously
Max stared at the
camera. Was this a
wind-up?

'Name?' repeated the
voice impatiently.

'Max. Max Barker, the pet sitter.'

'Welcome, Max Barker.'

There was a louder click, and a gate cleverly hidden in the fence swung open.

Max stared in amazement. 'Cool!' he said.

'Hurry up,' said the camera crossly. 'I haven't got all day.'

'Nor have I!' Max grabbed his bicycle and pushed it through the gate.

He was barely inside when the gate slammed shut and a second camera, mounted above the front door, focused its lens on him.

'Name?' said the camera, in a squeaky metallic voice.

'What? Again?'

'No name, no entry.'

'Max Barker. I'm here to pet–sit. I

thought this was an emergency!'

The front door opened so suddenly that Max almost fell inside.

'It is. Don't mind the cameras. They're a bit too enthusiastic at times. I'm Ivor. Thanks for coming so quickly.'

'Oh!' exclaimed Max, staring up.

Ivor Gadget was not the wrinkled old man Max had imagined. He was young and tall and wore his long brown hair loosely tied in a ponytail. Ivor glanced around, then quickly pulled Max inside, slamming the door behind him.

'Sorry about the security. I'm an inventor, if you hadn't already guessed. You wouldn't believe the trouble I've had with people trying to steal my ideas. But enough of me. Come and meet Dixie. You're going to love her!'

CHAPTER TWO
DIXIE VILLA

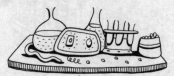

Max followed Ivor along the hall to a room at the back of the house. On the way he passed a lift-like door with a strip of red-and-white plastic tape stretched across it. A sign on the door read, 'Out of Order. Do NOT Enter.'

'What's that?' asked Max curiously. 'Is it a lift?'

Ivor looked shifty.

'Latest invention,' he mumbled. 'It's not finished.'

'What does it do?' asked Max.

Ivor stopped and turned to face him.

'No questions!' he said dramatically. 'Look, I'm going to have to ask you to sign the Ivor Gadget Secrecy Pact. Anything you see or hear about this house is strictly private. You mustn't tell anyone. Not an earwig!'

'I won't say a thing,' said Max, pretending to zip up his mouth. 'Am I signing in blood?'

'No need for that,' said Ivor. 'An ink pen will be fine. Providing it's not invisible ink of course!' He laughed.

Max laughed too. He'd only been joking about the blood!

'Here we are,' said Ivor, opening a door. 'Come and meet Dixie.'

Ivor ushered Max into the room. Max

stopped inside the door and stared in amazement. The room was even more messy than Alice's bedroom, and that was saying something! Tall bookcases lined the room and were crammed with everything from books to old bicycle wheels. The floor was covered with teetering piles of more books and mountains of cogs, wires, nuts, bolts, screws, computer bits and reels of sticky tape. Ivor wove his way through the junk to the table.

'Dixie Villa,' he said grandly.

'Wow!' Max exclaimed.

The cage looked like a two storey doll's house, but with a wire mesh front and a glass conservatory instead of a roof on top. Max peered through the mesh at the front rooms. Each one looked like an overgrown garden in miniature. The long grass was peppered with wild flowers, shaggy bushes and brambles. Max pushed his little finger through the mesh.

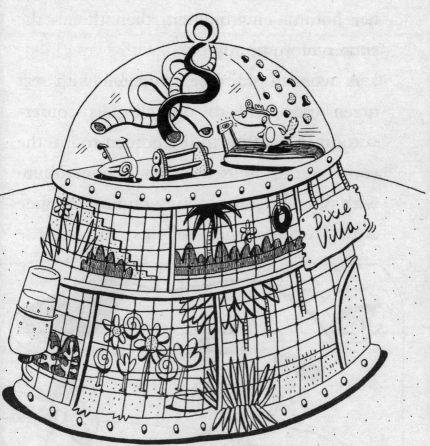

'Wicked!' he exclaimed. 'It's real.'

'Dixie likes the best of both words,' said Ivor, smiling at Max's astonishment. 'That's her natural environment, then there's the conservatory up top.'

A wooden staircase, carpeted with soft green moss, led to the all-glass conservatory. In contrast to the garden rooms the conservatory housed a huge gymnasium with three brightly coloured tunnels to slide down, a treadmill, weights, an exercise

bicycle and a climbing wall. A small dormouse, wearing green sweatbands around her head and paws, was pounding away on the treadmill. Suddenly the machine slowed, then it stopped and Dixie jumped off.

'Hello,' said Max, gently tapping on the glass.

Dixie fixed Max with her big black eyes. Then she turned her back on him.

'Dixie!' said Ivor, in a warning tone.

The little dormouse totally ignored him and hopped towards the stairs.

'Dixie,' said Ivor again, 'come and meet Max Barker, the pet sitter.'

Dixie reached the top of the staircase and hesitated.

'Max is going to look after you for the next three days. I know you don't want to stay here on your own, but it's not Max's fault so come and say hello.'

Ivor turned apologetically to Max, 'Dixie's not used to being locked inside her villa. Usually she comes and goes as she pleases.'

Dixie sat watching Ivor as if she was listening to him. When he'd finished she fluffed out her orange-brown fur and stared at Ivor with big eyes. Max held his breath. Dixie looked so sad he thought she might be going to cry!

'Dixie, don't!' Ivor pleaded. 'I've made up my mind – you're staying here while I go abroad.'

Dixie thumped her long furry tail on the ground, then, shooting an angry look at Max, she hopped down the staircase and out of sight.

'She likes me then!' said Max.

'It's not you,' said Ivor hurriedly. 'It's me she's cross with. I've never left her before and, as I said, I've never locked her up either.'

'I don't mind if you don't lock her cage,' said Max.

'It's not that simple,' said Ivor shiftily. 'Dixie's a live wire. She's always up to mischief. I don't want her messing with my inventions.'

He checked his watch.

'Widgets! Look at the time! I've got a plane to catch. I was lucky to get a seat – it was a last-minute cancellation. Quick, come to the kitchen. So much to do! There's the secrecy pact to sign, and your money to sort out. I'll show you what to feed Dixie and . . . Oops, I almost forgot! I need to do a scan of your eye.'

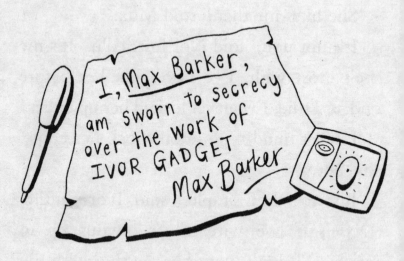

I, Max Barker,
am sworn to secrecy
over the work of
IVOR GADGET
Max Barker

CHAPTER THREE
A NASTY SHOCK

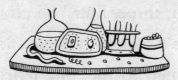

Cycling along to Ivor Gadget's early the next morning, Max reminded himself of his pet-sitting duties. Ivor had left all Dixie's favourite foods. There was a bag of hazelnuts, a jar of sunflower seeds, raspberries and apricots. It seemed an awful lot for such a small creature, but Ivor said that Dixie had a good appetite. Max had also brought Dixie a bunch of honeysuckle freshly cut from his garden. Last night, reading up about dormice, Max discovered they liked to shred it up and sleep in it. He hoped the present might cheer Dixie up. She hadn't seemed too happy yesterday.

Max reached the start of Ivor's fence and climbed off his bike.

'One, two, three, four,' he counted.

When he'd taken twelve footsteps he stopped, turned to face the fence and then counted six hands up from the bottom. Keeping his hand on the fence, Max crouched down until his eyes were level with his hand. Then, pulling it away, he stared at the fence. There it was! The tiny hole Ivor had told him about yesterday. There was a click, Max blinked and the hidden gate swung open.

'That is so neat!' Max exclaimed.

Instead of a key, the doors opened by recognizing people's eyes. Yesterday Ivor had scanned the inside of Max's eye so that he could get in too.

Leaving his bicycle just inside the gate Max repeated the whole thing at the front door shouting, 'Hi, Dixie. It's only me,' as he stepped inside.

The house had an empty feel. Maybe Dixie was still asleep. Max hurried down the hall, glancing curiously at the lift-like door as he passed. It was an odd thing to have in a home, and Max wondered what it was for. Pushing open the door to Dixie's room, Max threaded his way round the piles of junk. Dixie Villa seemed even more impressive this morning. Max decided Ivor must be very fond of the dormouse to build her such an amazing home. Dixie was not in the gym or any of the front rooms. Max lay the honeysuckle on the table in front of Dixie Villa and called out,

'Hi, Dixie. It's Max.'

Nothing, not even a friendly squeak! The silence worried Max.

'Dixie, are you in there? It's breakfast time. Come and say hello and then I'll get you something to eat. I wonder what you'd like? How about an apricot with some raspberries?'

There was still no sign of Dixie.

'Good choice. Apricot it is then,' said Max, reaching out to unclip the tiny water bottle fastened to the outside of Dixie's cage.

The bottle had a small metal drinking spout that poked through the cage bars.

Max was lifting it out when the spout whipped round and blasted him with cold water.

'Eeek!' he shrieked, dropping the bottle on the table. 'How the flip did that happen?' Wiping the water from his eyes, Max was sure he heard a squeaky giggle.

'Ouch!'

Something pinged him on the nose. It was

a sunflower seed and it was quickly followed by more. Max scrabbled around, picking them up and flicking them back. It was a waste of time. Dixie was too well hidden in the overgrown garden for the seeds to hit her, but Max enjoyed flicking the seeds all the same.

After a bit the missiles stopped. Over the top of a small bush came a twig with a white flower speared on the end.

'Truce,' shouted a squeaky voice.

Max stared in amazement as Dixie slowly peeked out from behind the bush.

126

A talking dormouse! Was this a trick too?

'Truce,' said Dixie crossly. 'Are you deaf or what?'

Max recovered himself.

'No, I just didn't realize that you could talk. You never said a word yesterday when Ivor was here.'

'There was nothing to say,' said Dixie. 'Truce? Will you stop fighting me?'

'You started it!' Max exclaimed.

'It's not my fault.'

'Well, it wasn't mine!'

'Being locked up is doing funny things to me. I'm going mad in here. You've got to let me out.'

Dixie's long black whiskers quivered. Max held his breath as she slowly edged out into the open. Her bright black eyes were sad, 'Please?' she said.

'Dixie, I can't do that. Ivor said I was to keep you locked up for your own safety.'

'Pooey!' exclaimed Dixie. 'I never mess with any of his inventions! Make them better, yes. Invent stuff Ivor's not even thought of, yes. But mess things up? No, NEVER!'

Max was torn. Dixie was used to having her freedom, and it felt mean to cage her, but Max was responsible for her safety. What if he disobeyed Ivor and something went wrong – how would he feel then?

'It's only for three days. You'll be out before you know it. I'll spend the daytime with you, if you like. Keep you company.'

'Pooey! I'd rather keep my own company,' Dixie growled.

'Suit yourself,' said Max. 'The offer stands, if you change your mind. I'll get your breakfast.'

He picked up the water bottle from the table.

'Neat trick, by the way. How did you get it to squirt me?'

Dixie didn't answer. Sighing to himself, Max took the bottle along to the kitchen to refill it. Ivor had left the apricots in a bowl and Max gently squeezed them, choosing the softest for Dixie's breakfast. He cut it in half, removed the stone and piled fresh raspberries on top. The whole thing looked so tasty that Max could have eaten it himself. He washed his sticky hands before proudly carrying the water and food back to Dixie.

'Breakfast, and I brought you some honeysuckle too.'

Max hadn't expected an answer, but when he looked through the cage he got a nasty shock. Dixie lay on her side in the long grass, eyes closed, tail stuck out like a flag pole. She was very still. Too still. Max stepped closer.

CHAPTER FOUR

THE CHASE

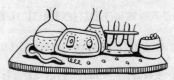

'**D**ixie? Dixie, are you all right?'

Max threw down her breakfast and wrenched open the front of the cage. A jumble of thoughts whizzed through his mind. Dixie was so still she didn't seem to be breathing. Had she died? But how? She'd been fine a few minutes ago. Unless the upset had given her a heart attack. Max thought he was having one too. His heart was jumping like a kangaroo. What should he do? Last term at school, Max's class had been taught how to give mouth-to-mouth resuscitation. It was a way of breathing for someone if they couldn't do it for themselves. Could you give a dormouse mouth-to-mouth? Max decided to try. He knew to be careful. Dixie was so little that if he breathed too hard she might blow up like a balloon!

Dixie lay stone still as with trembling fingers Max reached inside the cage to lift her out. His fingers touched her thick orange fur. Thwap! Dixie smacked Max with her tail.

'Sucker!' she squeaked, jumping up and leaping to freedom.

'Dixie!' bellowed Max. 'That's not funny.'

Dixie scampered across the table, scattering the bunch of honeysuckle as she ran down to the floor. Max leaped after her, knocking over piles of junk in his rush to stop her from escaping. He would have caught her if he hadn't tripped over a broken guitar that sent him crashing to the ground.

'Mouse brains!' said Max, pulling his foot from the hole in the middle. The guitar's broken strings snaked round his legs, holding him tightly. Max pulled them away, then scrambled after Dixie. He was in time to see her fat orange tail disappear around the bend in the stairs. Max climbed up after her and found himself in a room even more cluttered than the one he'd just left.

'Dixie?'

Max leaned against the door frame and scanned the messy room. And his mum thought she had problems with Alice! You could hide a rhinoceros in here and nobody would ever know.

'Come on, Dixie. The joke's over.'

Dixie didn't answer. No surprises there then!

There was another lift-like door in this room, with a single strip of red-and-white plastic tape across it. Max did some quick calculating. It was directly above the one downstairs. So it was a lift! He noticed a

keypad to the side of the door, with two large buttons marked P and F. What did that mean? Max grinned. Inventors! They were all the same. Two cakes short of a party!

There was a rustle from the other side of the room. Max spun around. The noise had come from under the window. Silently he tiptoed towards it. Suddenly an orange ball of fur broke cover and shot across the room towards the door. Turning, Max dived, his fingers closing around Dixie's tail as he landed.

'Gotcha!'

But he hadn't! Max was left holding a clump of soft orange fur as Dixie scampered away. There followed a crazy chase – Dixie whizzing around the room, Max crashing after her through mounds of junk. Max was determined to catch Dixie and dived like a footballer each time the dormouse popped into sight. A bead of sweat ran down his nose, and his heart was banging like mad. He paused for a moment to catch his

breath, then leaped
up as Dixie shot past.
Halfway across the
room Dixie disappeared in
a bundle of old clothes.
The clothes jumped and
wriggled like live things, then suddenly
stopped moving. Max crept closer. A stripy
jumper caught his eye. Was that a
dormouse-shaped bump in its sleeve?
Silently Max squatted down. Yes, he was
sure it was Dixie! Max prodded the bump.
The jumper squeaked and the bump ran
down its sleeve. Max cupped
his hands and as Dixie ran
out through the cuff he
sprang.

'Gotcha!' he cried.
He skidded across

the floor, crashed through the red plastic tape and smacked into the lift buttons. The lift door sprang open and Max hurtled inside, letting Dixie go as he rolled across the floor. Dixie struggled up, then stared around in horror.

'Quick!' she squeaked. 'We've got to get out of here!'

The lift doors were closing.

Dixie ran towards them shrieking, 'Out, NOW!'

Max could see they wouldn't make it in time so he looked for a button to keep the doors open. All lifts had them, so where was it? He ran his hands across the wall in case he was missing something and found a crease in the surface. He felt it with his finger. The crease made a square with an indent at the top. Max stuck his finger into the indent and pulled. The square of wall opened, revealing the lift's controls: four buttons and a circular hole with a wire poking out. The buttons were marked with P, F, <> and ><. The symbols were the same as the ones in the lift at the shopping centre. Max couldn't guess what the P and F meant but he knew that <> would open the doors and >< would close them.

The lift doors snapped shut. Frantically Max pushed the button marked <> but it was too late. The lift was moving.

CHAPTER FIVE

A RIDE IN A LIFT

They were going up, which was strange as Ivor's house only had two floors. After a few seconds the lift stopped. Relieved, Max pressed the button to open the doors, and when nothing happened he pressed it again. Without warning the lift threw itself sideways. Max grabbed for the handrail and was glad he had. Now the lift was spinning, faster and faster, making his skinny body shake and his teeth chatter together.

'Hold on,' shouted Dixie, climbing on to

Max's foot and sinking her claws into his shoelace.

'Great idea!' said Max, like he was going to do anything else! He was spinning so violently that he could hardly breathe. He wanted to pick Dixie up, make sure she was safe, but when he tried he found the force was too great and he couldn't move.

The spinning went on until Max could hardly bear it, then at last the lift slowed and finally stopped moving. 'Whoa!' said Max. He stood for a

second, too giddy to move, but then as he reached up to open the doors . . .

'Eek!'

Faster than a stone hurled from the top of a tower block, the lift plummeted. Max's stomach met his feet, then suddenly, without even slowing, the lift stopped again. Max almost bit his tongue as it bounced up and down like it had landed on an enormous trampoline. Up and down went the lift, until gradually it stopped and the doors slid open.

'Dixie, are you OK?'

There was a muffled squeak. Dixie was clinging on to Max's shoelace with her teeth as well as both his front paws. Max

142

staggered through the doors blinking in the bright light. 'That,' he said, 'was some ride!'

'Don't mind me,' Dixie squeaked crossly. She jumped from Max's foot. 'Call yourself a pet sitter! You nearly squashed me with those thumping great feet.'

'Sorry!' Max bent down to pick her up, but she slapped him off with her tail.

'You will be,' she exclaimed. 'Ivor's going to kill you when he finds out you've taken his lift. You're the one that needs locking up. Not me!'

'What! This is your fault!' said Max hotly. 'I'm only here because I was chasing you. Where are we, anyway? Is this Ivor's garden?'

He looked around and saw neatly trimmed hedges, colourful plants, stone statues, a rectangular pond with a dolphin fountain in the middle and mosaic around the edge.

'Nice,' said Max, 'if you like that sort of thing. Bit too Ancient Rome for me. There's nowhere to kick a ball.'

'Ancient Rome?' asked Dixie.

'Yep, we did it in history last term. We had a Roman Britain day and wore tunics a bit like that boy over there . . .' Max's voice trailed away.

'Hide,' hissed Dixie, diving under a bush.

Max wriggled after her. The boy was in a hurry and luckily didn't notice the lift nestled between two small willowy trees. He muttered to himself as he struggled to carry a huge basket full of ripe cherries. Max's stomach rumbled. Breakfast seemed a long time ago.

Dixie, who hadn't eaten her breakfast, was

obviously thinking the same thing. 'Come on,' she said, once the boy had passed. 'Let's go and find where those cherries came from.'

'Hang on!' said Max. 'Dixie, where are we exactly?'

'Not too sure,' said Dixie. 'Roman Britain sounds about right. Impossible to say without looking at the time dial.'

'You're saying that's a time lift!' squeaked Max. 'I don't believe you!'

'Excuse me, did I say time lift? Silly me! I meant we've taken the lift to Ivor's attic. Look around, bright eyes. What do you see?'

Max stuck his head out of the bush and gazed around, noticing a low villa with high windows and a veranda on the other side of the pond. Just then two girls in short white tunics hurried up the garden with a basket of tomatoes and disappeared inside the house.

'It is Roman Britain!' Max exclaimed. 'Unreal!'

'Well I'm real and I need food,' said Dixie. 'Come on.'

Max hesitated. The responsible pet-sitter

side of him said to get back into the lift and go straight home. But the curious, adventure-seeking side was dying to see a bit more of Roman Britain.

'Hurry up,' said Dixie. 'You'll think better on a full stomach.'

Max crumpled. The cherries had looked delicious. Surely it wouldn't hurt to have a little look around? It was the chance of a lifetime, and he'd regret it if he didn't take it. He scrambled out of the bush and hurried after Dixie.

'What did you mean about thinking better on a full stomach?' he asked.

Dixie didn't answer and Max got the feeling she was hiding something, but before

he could question her they reached the orchard.

'Wow!' said Max, impressed by the fruit-laden trees. 'Where shall we start?'

CHAPTER SIX

DIXIE DISAPPEARS

A short ladder was propped against one tree, and next to it was a huge basket full of shiny red cherries. Dixie scampered up the side of the basket and began eating. Max had never picked cherries before so he climbed halfway up the ladder and ate them straight from the tree. They tasted delicious! Sticky sweet juice squirted over him as he bit into the soft flesh. He was so busy eating, and seeing how far he could spit the stones, that he didn't hear the soft steps approaching. He nearly fell off the

ladder in surprise when a voice shouted up at him,

'Don't let the master catch you. He'll chop your hand off for that.'

Max's stomach clenched. Suddenly the fruit tasted sour in his mouth.

'You're new, aren't you? Where are you from? You must be foreign with clothes like that!'

'I'm not the one wearing the dress!' Max exclaimed.

The boy gave him an odd look.

'There's no need to be unfriendly.'

'I wasn't,' said Max, trying not to laugh.

Max always laughed

152

when he was nervous, and it often got him into trouble. 'I'm British,' he added.

'You must be from up north then. I hear they're a barbaric lot up there. Were you caught trying to cross Hadrian's Wall?' asked the boy sympathetically.

Max was wondering how to answer when the boy added, 'Enough of the chatter! There's no time for idleness with a banquet to prepare. Come. You can give me a hand with the basket. It's needed in the kitchen.'

Max stared at the boy. What should he do? He didn't want to go to the kitchen, where there would be lots of people and more chance of discovery. Slowly, as he backed down the ladder, a simple plan formed in his head. He would grab Dixie and make a run for it back to the lift. But Dixie had disappeared. Max stared at the basket. Was she hiding among the cherries or had she climbed out and gone somewhere else?

'Hurry up,' said the boy. 'We'll get a beating if we're too long.'

There was nothing for it. Max took one handle of the basket and reluctantly helped the boy to carry it back to the kitchen. He needn't have worried about being discovered. The kitchen was hot and crowded, with too many people all rushing around.

'Put that there, then go fetch me some lettuce,' snapped a hassled-looking cook wearing a three-quarters-length tunic. 'And be quick.'

Max stared at the basket of cherries. This was a good chance to escape, but where was Dixie? Max couldn't leave without the dormouse.

'I'm going to the garden to get some lettuce,' he said loudly, in case Dixie was in the basket and could hear him.

The cook eyed him suspiciously.

'Just get on with it,' she snapped.

Max stared at the basket once more and saw that the cherries were moving. They rolled over each other like glossy red marbles as something pushed its way through them. A twitchy nose followed by long whiskers appeared.

'About time too,' said Max, bending

down and scooping Dixie into his hand. 'Been enjoying yourself, have you?'

'Keep your tail on,' said Dixie. 'It was no picnic in there.'

'No?' Max chuckled, wiping a smear of cherry juice from Dixie's face. 'Course it wasn't.'

'Oi,' shouted a short girl in a dirty tunic, pointing an accusing finger at Max. 'The new boy's got a fatty mouse. He stole it from the pot.'

'Fatty mouse! Huh!' squeaked Dixie, indignantly.

Max burst out laughing, but the kitchen fell silent and everyone stared at him. Bang! The hassled-looking cook slammed her knife into the table.

'No one steals from my kitchen,' she roared. 'Here, boy, now!'

'Stealing?' Max shot a furious look at the

girl in the grubby tunic. 'I wasn't stealing. I caught a dormouse eating the cherries and I was putting her outside.'

'Why?' asked the cook, staring at Max.

Max returned her gaze without even blinking. 'Because that's where she belongs.'

'You're new, aren't you? Then I'll give you the benefit of the doubt. Give me the fatty mouse. It belongs in this pot.'

Max let out a tiny sigh of relief as the cook pointed to a large clay pot high on a shelf. Max's brain buzzed as he tried to remember why the Ancient Romans would keep dormice in a clay pot.

'Galloping gladiators!' he hissed, suddenly recalling the reason.

Dormice, or fatty mice as

they called them, were a delicacy in Roman times. They were kept in clay pots until they were nice and plump, then they were cooked. If he handed Dixie over, she would be roasted and eaten at the banquet. Max closed his hand protectively around his little friend. Stroppy as she was, he couldn't help liking her. Besides, he was the pet sitter. There was no way he was handing over his latest responsibility.

'Hurry, boy,' snapped the woman.

'I'll put her back,' said Max, stalling for time.

'You! You're far too short to reach.' The woman laughed. 'Give the fatty mouse here, then go and fetch the lettuce.'

Max started towards her then suddenly he gave a blood-curdling yell and gently dropped Dixie on the floor.

'Ouch! She bit me!'

Clutching his finger, Max gave an award-winning performance of pretending to be in pain.

'Clumsy oaf!' shrieked the cook. 'Don't just stand there. Catch it!'

Dirty Tunic took off, shoving past Max to chase after Dixie.

'Snitch,' Max muttered, thinking he'd like to shove her in a pot for roasting.

Several of the younger slaves also downed

their tools to join in the chase, while the older ones shook their heads and carried on working. Desperately Max elbowed people out of the way. He had to reach Dixie before anyone else did. But Dixie was whizzing around and around the kitchen like a firecracker and no one could get near her. She darted across the feet of a boy who then slipped on a tomato and crashed to the ground. A second boy tripped over him, pulling Dirty Tunic down with him.

'Wicked!' cheered Max, avoiding the pile-up.

Dixie squeezed behind a tall clay jar as the slaves on the floor struggled to get up.

'Where did it go?'

'It was there a minute ago.'

'It went that way.'

Max sidled over to the jar and squatted down beside it.

'Dixie,' he hissed, 'it's me. Max. Climb on to my hand and I'll get you out of here.'

'No,' said Dixie hotly. 'There's a whole bunch of my relatives in that pot. I'm not leaving without freeing them.'

'You're not going to try and rescue them? Dixie, you can't! It's far too dangerous. We have to get back to the lift before there's real trouble.'

'Go without me then.'

'Don't tempt me,' said Max.

'I'm not going anywhere until I've saved my relations,' said Dixie. 'You wouldn't.'

Max thought about his relatives, and an image of Alice making fun of him in front of all her friends floated into his head. Would he risk his life to save Alice? Annoying as she was, Max knew he probably would.

'All right,' he said. 'Climb on my hand and I'll help you rescue them.'

CHAPTER SEVEN

STUCK IN TIME

Dixie clambered into Max's hand and he closed his fingers around her soft little body. Half a second later he was surrounded by Dirty Tunic and a bunch of slaves.

'Where did the mouse go?' asked one. 'Did you see it?'

'It went that way,' said Max.

He chuckled as the slaves rushed to the other side of the kitchen, then casually he sauntered over to the shelf where the earthenware pot stood. No one noticed. The older slaves were busy with their work. The younger ones were searching for Dixie in a basket of tomatoes. Max pulled himself up on to the wooden table directly below the shelf. The table wobbled, and Max grabbed at the shelf to steady himself. The clay pot was heavy and Max needed both hands to lift it down. He was so busy trying not to drop it that when the table wobbled again Max fell back, landing on his bottom with the clay pot in his lap. His hand flew to his pocket and felt for Dixie, then he grinned as she tickled him with her tail. That was close. He'd have to be more careful. The jar would have given Dixie more than a headache if it had landed on her!

Dirty Tunic was crawling around on the floor. If she looked up now she would see Max sitting on the table. Quietly Max lay the jar on its side and eased the lid off. He angled the jar away from himself, expecting the dormice to rush out, but nothing happened. Max stuck his hand inside the jar and his fingers sank into a mass of velvety bodies. Even then they didn't stir.

'Dixie, help me,' Max whispered.

Dixie wriggled out of his pocket, climbed on to the jar and stuck her head inside. She began squeaking very fast in dormouse language. Seconds later the jar erupted with orange fur balls as a dozen fat dormice scampered to safety. As

they fled they knocked the lid to the ground and it smashed on the stone floor. Dirty Tunic spun round.

'You!' she cried, standing up. 'You've let all the fatty mice go.'

Max grabbed Dixie and scrambled down from the table, but the cook had seen him.

'Clumsy!' she yelled, boxing Max on the ear. 'Catch them now or I'll be roasting you instead.'

Max fled across the kitchen and outside. Dirty Tunic followed as Max dodged around the statues to the part of the garden where they'd left the lift.

'Stop!' cried Dirty Tunic.

'In your dreams,' shouted Max.

The lift was where he'd remembered – sandwiched between two willowy trees. Max threw himself at it, slamming his hand

on the buttons outside. The doors slid open.
Max ran in, flipped open the hidden control
panel and pressed the >< button.

'Hooray!' he cheered as the lift closed.

'What is this place?' asked a voice.

Max spun round. Dirty Tunic had
followed him into the lift.

'Get out,' he said, shoving her backwards.

'Shan't.'

'Get out!' yelled Max, shoving her harder.

Dirty Tunic leaned against the lift doors. 'I can't. The door's disappeared. This place is so strange.'

'Bye-bye,' said Max.

He pushed a button, the doors slid open and Dirty Tunic fell backwards into the garden.

'You can't hide in there forever,' she shouted as the doors closed again.

Max slumped against the lift wall to catch his breath.

'Dixie, what do we press to get home?' he asked. 'Is it the F button? F for future, right?'

169

Dixie crouched on the floor and her long black whiskers trembled.

'It's not that simple,' she said.

'Well, make it simple,' yelled Max. 'We haven't got much time.'

Dixie quivered. 'I can't. I was going to tell you earlier.'

'Tell me what?' Max felt uneasy. What hadn't Dixie told him?

'We can't get back. The lift isn't finished. The time dial needs a pointer so you can pick the exact date you want to travel to. Ivor's friend Tor was making a special one carved from oak. Ivor was so excited when Tor emailed to say that the pointer was ready. That's why he went away, to collect the pointer.'

Max stared at Dixie in disbelief. After a minute he asked, 'So how did we get here?'

'Pot luck,' Dixie replied. 'Pressing F takes you somewhere into the future. Pressing P takes you back into the past. You just can't set an exact date.'

'Nice!' exploded Max. 'Why didn't you tell this me before?'

'You were more interested in going off to find the cherries,' said Dixie.

'What! The cherries were your idea.' Max's green eyes narrowed to tiny slits.

'All right!' said Dixie sounding a tiny bit embarrassed. 'I decided to keep it for later. I think better on a full stomach.'

Max felt his heart beat faster as he thought about their predicament. They could be stuck in the wrong time forever.

'OK!' he said slowly. His heart was still racing and he felt slightly out of breath. 'What happens now?'

'We press the F button and hope for the best. Wherever we go, it can't be worse than this place,' Dixie shuddered. 'Roasted dormouse! That's bad!'

It wasn't the answer Max wanted, but Dixie was right. Travelling nearer to their own time had to be less dangerous than being stuck in Ancient Roman times. Then

Max had an idea. What if they had a makeshift time-dial pointer? Might that get them back to their own time?

'What does the pointer look like? Could we make one?'

'It's got a round bottom and a long pointy stick like a speed dial in a car,' said Dixie.

Max glanced at Dixie's fat little body and her long tail, then grinned.

'No way!' squeaked Dixie, reading his mind. 'You are not using me!' A sudden pounding on the door made Max and Dixie jump.

'Open up!' bellowed a man's voice.

The pounding continued until the lift doors burst open. A surprised–looking man in a long white tunic stared in. Dirty Tunic was with him, and she was fiddling with the lift controls.

'That's him,' she said, smugly.

Quickly Max pushed the >< button and the doors slid closed again. He kept his finger on the button to keep them shut, ignoring the angry shouts from outside.

Think! What could you use for a makeshift time-dial pointer? Unusually Max's pockets were empty except for his pet sitter's notebook and pencil. Max stared around the lift, but apart from himself and Dixie it was completely empty. Then he had an idea. His pencil would make a good pointer and the button on his trousers was round! Using his free hand Max unfastened his button and tried to pull it off. The button was stitched so firmly in place that it didn't even move.

'Dixie,' said Max, 'can you nibble this free for me?'

'Good idea,' said Dixie. 'You're going to use it for a pointer.'

Quickly she scampered up Max's leg and sunk her teeth into the cotton. Max giggled.

'That tickles!'

The pounding on the door grew more violent.

'Open up. Open up at once or I'll feed you to the lions!'

'Careful!' chuckled Max. 'Your whiskers are soooo tickly!'

'Paaa!' Dixie spat a mouthful of cotton, then triumphantly passed Max the button. 'It goes in that hole,' she said.

'I know,' said Max, having already worked out that the hole in the control panel was where the time-dial pointer should be.

Max threaded the button through the dangling wire with his free hand. It was far too small, but it would have to do. Next he fastened the pencil to it, using the end of the wire. He gave it a twist, cheering as the pencil spun around.

'Ready?' he asked Dixie.

'Ready,' she agreed, climbing into his pocket.

Max thought for a

moment. He wasn't sure how far to turn the pencil. Roman times had been around two thousand years ago, so he'd better give it a good twist. The pounding outside was replaced by a metallic-sounding twang as if someone was attacking the lift with an axe. Hurriedly Max turned the pencil three-quarters of the way round, then slammed his hand on the F button. For a second nothing happened, then the lift suddenly shot sideways then upwards.

'Hooray!' cheered Max, grabbing the handrail as the spinning began.

CHAPTER EIGHT
INTO THE FUTURE

The spinning lasted for longer this time. Max gripped the rail until his hands were numb from holding on. He could feel Dixie's warm little body in his pocket, and he hoped that she was all right. When at last the spinning stopped, Max waited, ready for the sudden plunge downwards. But the time lift was full of surprises.

'Eeeek!' he shouted as they shot upwards.

Max wasn't sure which was worse: the feeling of falling or this new feeling of whizzing into space. Neither, he decided. It was this bit: the sudden jolt as the lift

178

bounced itself to a standstill. This was a hundred times worse than anything else. Max's bones felt as if they were about to come crashing through his skin. He closed his eyes until at last the lift stilled and the doors finally slid open.

'Phew!' he cried, seeing they were downstairs in Ivor's hall. 'We made it! How lucky was that?'

Eagerly Dixie scrambled from Max's pocket.

'Listen!' Max caught her as she scampered down his leg. 'What's that noise?'

Cautiously he stuck his head out of the lift, then quickly pulled it back in. Who was the old man with the long grey hair shuffling down the hall? Ivor hadn't said that anyone else would be visiting Dixie.

Coughing and wheezing, the man shuffled closer.

'Who's there?' he called. 'I thought I heard something.

Who is it?'

'Ivor!' squeaked Dixie. 'What happened?'

Something clicked in Max's brain.

'Dozy dormice!' he exclaimed. 'We've overshot. We've travelled into the future.'

Quickly he shut the lift doors, then reaching up he twisted the pencil back a little and hit the Past button.

'Let's hope this does it,' he muttered as the lift began to spin.

Anxiously Max waited. What if he'd turned the pointer too far? They could be travelling backwards and forwards forever. Seconds later the ride was over and the lift doors opened. Tentatively Max looked out.

They were back in Ivor's house, in the upstairs room they had started from. 'We did it! We're home!' Max cheered. He checked his watch – they'd been gone an hour, although it seemed much longer. Hitching up his shorts, which were slipping down his skinny waist, he triumphantly carried Dixie out of the lift.

CHAPTER NINE
HOME AGAIN

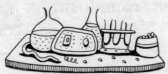

Max and Dixie were having a water fight with Dixie's water bottles. Dixie had shown Max how to make the spout twist around and squirt water, but she was still getting the better of him as she was expert at hiding.

'Mouse-eye!' shouted Dixie, leaping from behind a tyre and blasting Max in the face.

'I'll get you for that,' laughed Max, wiping water from his eyes.

'Not if I get you first,' shrieked Dixie, blasting Max again.

Max ducked and fired back, soaking Dixie's long furry tail as she nipped behind an old computer.

'Mouse-eye!' he yelled.

'Hold fire!' Dixie's head popped round the computer, her ears twitching.

'Yeah, right!' laughed Max, blasting her again. 'I'm not that stupid!'

'No, really. That was the door. Quick, Ivor's home!'

Dixie ran back to her cage. Max dropped his water bottle and frantically mopped up the mess. He managed to clear up most of the water before Ivor came in to the room.

'Hello,' said Max, stuffing a wad of wet tissue into his pocket.

'Hello,' said Ivor, looking around. 'It's a bit damp in here. Is everything all right?'

'Everything's fine,' said Max.

'Couldn't be finer,' called Dixie from her villa.

Ivor looked at them both suspiciously.

'Good to see you two so friendly,' he said eventually. 'Dixie behaved herself, did she? She wasn't talking to you when I left.'

'Dixie's been very good,' said Max.

'What about him?' Ivor looked at Dixie.

'The best pet sitter ever,' said Dixie.

'I knew he would be.' Ivor dumped his suitcase on top of the broken guitar, then let Dixie out of her cage.

'Did you have an enjoyable trip?' asked Max politely.

'Oh yes,' Ivor's eyes flicked to his suitcase. 'The trip went very well. The time just flew by. I can't believe I've been away for three whole days. I'll be an old man, little and bald, before I know it.'

Max and Dixie chuckled.

'Old maybe, but bald . . . I don't think so.' Dixie winked at Max.

Ivor tweaked his long ponytail.

'Maybe not bald,' he agreed.

'Old and grey?' suggested Max.

Ivor gave him a sharp look, but Max was already hurrying for the door.

'I'll be off then,' he called. 'See you around Dixie. Bye Ivor.'

'Bye Max,' said Dixie. 'See you sometime in the future, maybe!'

Me and Dixie!

The Pet Sitter

PARROT PANDEMONIUM

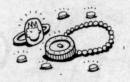

For Sarah, Diane and Jill – J.S.
For Ella Rose – N.R.

CONTENTS

CHAPTER ONE
ANOTHER JOB

Max was on his way out to the garden when the telephone rang.

'I'll get it,' he said.

'It'll be for you anyway,' said Mum. 'It always is.'

Max snatched up the phone and was nearly deafened by the person on the other end.

'Is that Max Barker?'

'Yes,' said Max, hoping this was another job. Max was a pet sitter. He loved animals, but couldn't have any of his own because his big sister Alice was allergic to them.

'Hi, Max. My name's Captain Boom. I need a pet sitter to look after Squawk, my parrot. I'm going away tomorrow for two days, so could you come and meet him now?'

'Sure,' said Max, sticking his tongue out at Alice as she shoved past him. 'Where do you live?'

'At the Blue Water Marina, on a boat

called the *Leaky Dip*. You can't miss it. It's the oldest thing here apart from me.' Captain Boom laughed. 'How long will it take you to get here?'

'Ten minutes,' said Max.

'See you in ten minutes then,' said Captain Boom, hanging up.

Max quickly wrote Captain Boom's details in his pet sitter's notebook, then pulled on his trainers.

'Going somewhere?' asked Mum.

'Yes,' said Max. 'To the Blue Water Marina to meet Captain Boom. He wants me to look after his parrot.'

'But you don't know anything about parrots,' said Mum.

'I do,' Max replied. 'Alice is like a parrot. She squawks a lot and she's always repeating herself.'

'Muuuum! Tell him off!' squawked Alice.

Max grinned. 'See what I mean! Bye, Mum. Bye, Alice.'

'Be back by five,' called Mrs Barker.

As Max cycled to the marina he tried to imagine what Captain Boom would be like. He had a very loud voice for an old person. Would Squawk be old too? Max imagined an elderly bird with faded eyes and hardly any feathers.

'Pretty Polly,' he chirped, imitating the parrot in the local pet shop.

It didn't take long for Max to find the *Leaky Dip*. Captain Boom had been right; his boat was definitely the oldest one at the marina. Chaining his bike to a mooring ring, Max eyed the *Leaky Dip*'s gangplank. It was falling to pieces and didn't look very safe. Carefully he stepped on to it. The

gangplank creaked and Max waited a moment before taking another step forward. He was just taking a third step when someone bellowed, 'STOP!'

The voice was so fierce that Max immediately froze.

'Put your hands in the air.'

Max raised his arms. The rickety gangplank wobbled and he stared ahead, fixing his gaze on the *Leaky Dip*'s main mast to stop himself from losing his balance and falling into the sea.

'Walk forward, nice and slow. That's it. Now, lie face down on the deck.'

'What?' exclaimed Max. 'No way! I . . .'

'Do it!' roared the voice. 'Or I'll blow you to the other side of the world with a cannonball.'

CHAPTER TWO

ON BOARD THE *LEAKY DIP*

Max did as he was told, feeling his pet sitter's notebook slide out of his pocket as he lay down. He wanted to pick it up but he didn't dare. Being blown to the other side of the world wasn't on his agenda. Not today.

'Who are you?' snarled the voice. 'Why were you sneaking up my gangplank?'

'I'm Max Barker. I'm the pet sitter,' said Max, as clearly as he could with his mouth squashed against the deck's dusty surface.

'Of course you are!' said a deeper and much more friendly voice. 'Shiver me shoes, are you all right? I've been meaning to fix that gangplank for ages. Did you trip over the loose bit?'

Two strong hands hauled Max to his feet, and he found himself staring up at a huge man with bright blue eyes, a curly black beard and one hooped earring. Captain Boom must have been joking on the phone. He wasn't old at all and looked every bit a pirate. He was dressed in a white shirt, gold-buttoned waistcoat and raggedy three-quarter length trousers.

'Captain Billy Boom,' he said,

shaking Max's hand. 'Thanks for coming so quickly, and I'm really sorry about that gangplank. I'll fix it before I go, and that's a promise.'

'Er, great,' said Max, staring around to see who the other voice belonged to.

But apart from Captain Boom the deck was empty.

'Weird!' muttered Max, sure he hadn't imagined the other voice.

He rescued his notebook and flicked through until he found the right page.

'Captain Boom, the *Leaky Dip*, Blue Water Marina. Your parrot's called Squawk and you're going away for two days.'

'S'right.' Captain Boom sighed. 'It's Treasure trouble.'

'Bad luck,' said Max sympathetically.

'Did you forget where you buried it?'

Captain Boom roared with laughter.

'Not treasure,' he spluttered. 'Wish it was though. No, I'm going to visit Treasure. She's my sister, and believe me when I say she's trouble!'

'So is my big sister, Alice,' said Max. 'Is Treasure your big sister too?'

'You could say that. Think whale, then double it,' chuckled Captain Boom. 'But enough of Treasure. Come and meet Squawk.'

Captain Boom led the way across the deck, behind the mast and up five steps to the quarterdeck. Max followed, weaving his way around piles of frayed ropes, tattered sails and one very rusty cannon.

''Scuse the mess,' said Captain Boom. 'It never used to be like this. The clutter built up when the old boat sprung so many leaks that I had to stop sailing in her. I'll have a tidy up before I go, and that's a promise.'

Captain Boom stopped at a woody mast a bit smaller than the *Leaky Dip*'s main one and bellowed:

'Squawk, Max is here. Come down and say hello.'

Max squinted upwards and quickly realized something.

'That's not a mast; it's a tree!'

The tree looked like it had come straight from a tropical rainforest. Max ran his hand across its bark expecting it to be a fake, but the tree was real.

'Squawk,' shouted Captain Boom, 'come and meet Max.'

Shielding his eyes from the sun, Max stared between the tree's feathery leaves, hoping to catch a glimpse of Squawk. Nothing. The parrot stayed hidden.

'That's so cool!' said Max. 'A real tree growing on a

boat. I bet Squawk loves it.'

'S'right,' said Captain Boom. 'I got it when I got Squawk. Parrots and trees go together like sea and sand, maps and treasure, sharks and . . . SQUAWK! Get down from there right now. Don't think I can't see you!'

There was an angry screech from behind Max. He wheeled round in time to see a red blur hurtling towards him from the rigging of the main mast.

'Duck!' roared Captain Boom.

'It's not. It's definitely a parrot,' shouted Max, covering his head with his hands as the feathered cannonball hurtled closer.

CHAPTER THREE
SQUAWK SPEAKS

'**S**quawk, STOP!' roared Captain Boom. 'That's NOT funny. Behave yourself or I'll throw you in the bilge!'

The bird stopped mid-dive, skidding to a halt about a metre above the captain's head. Then, flying very slowly, he landed on Captain Boom's shoulder.

'Nice emergency stop,' said Max, impressed.

'Max, meet Squawk,' Captain Boom lightly stroked his parrot's beak. 'And, Squawk, meet Max, your pet sitter.'

'Hello, Squawk,' said Max.

Squawk fluffed up
his magnificent red, blue
and yellow feathers, then
stuck his beak in the air.

'Squawk,' said Captain Boom
with a note of warning, 'say hello to Max.'

Reluctantly Squawk fixed Max with his
small, black eyes.

'M . . . A . . . T,' he said, slowly. 'M-A-T.
Hello, Mat.'

'Max,' said Max and Captain Boom,
together.

'Mat,' repeated Squawk stubbornly.

'It's Max!' yelled Captain Boom.

'Mat,' said Squawk, giving Max a
hard stare. 'Mat. Cat. Cat, mat. The cat sat
on Mat.'

Max laughed.

'Very good,' he chuckled. 'A talking

parrot with a sense of humour.'

'Squawk's got a sense of humour all right,' said Captain Boom drily. 'And as for talking, he could talk the mainsail right off its mast. Ouch! Don't bite my ear. And while we're on the don'ts . . .' Captain Boom paused to make sure both Squawk and Max were listening. 'Don't let Squawk go anywhere near the mast. He loves it up there, but he's banned because he's a menace. He fiddles with the rigging and that causes accidents. And please DON'T upset my neighbour, Captain Becky Bones.'

Captain Boom pointed to a smart boat moored a short distance from the *Leaky Dip*. A skull and crossbones flew from each of its three masts, but not the usual type of skull and crossbones. Each of the skulls on Captain Becky Bones's flags had red blood oozing from their eye sockets. Max shivered and wished that Becky's boat was moored somewhere a bit further away, like Australia.

'Becky Bones, Captain of the *Shark's Teeth* and terror of the seas,' whispered Captain Boom. 'Upset her at your peril!'

Squawk crossed his eyes and made a gagging sound as if someone was strangling him.

Captain Boom grinned.

'And she'd have you for parrot pie too,' he said cheerfully. 'Right then, Max, let's step below and I'll show you what Squawk likes to eat.'

Leaving Squawk in his tree, Captain Boom climbed down a creaky ladder from the main deck. The space downstairs was even messier than up top. Gingerly Max followed the captain through a large cabin with a squashy sofa and small television and on into a tiny kitchen.

'This is the galley,' Captain Boom proudly announced.

Max squeezed in after him, nose wrinkled, expecting the worst, but the galley was spotlessly clean and tidy. Cooking utensils dangled from hooks on the wall, silver pans hung over a tiny cooker, and strings of garlic and onions hung around the porthole.

'I love cooking,' explained Captain Boom, patting his massive stomach. 'And Squawk and I both love eating.'

He pulled open a cupboard door and Max stared in amazement. The shelves were full of plastic containers, all neatly labelled in black pen.

'Walnuts, brazils, pecans, cashews,' read Max. 'Wheat, maize, sunflower, oats, linseed.'

'Squawk likes variety,' said Captain Boom, pulling open another door to reveal a fridge stashed with oranges, apples, grapes, cherries, mangoes, kiwi fruit, carrots, beans and much more. 'I'll write you a menu for each day. Make sure he has plenty of fresh water, and at bedtime he gets a treat of toast covered in honey, then cut into fingers and dipped in tea.'

'Not much then!' joked Max. 'Perhaps I'll move in here. All I get at bedtime is a lecture on cleaning my teeth.'

'Feel free,' said Captain Boom. 'I'll make a bunk up for you in the spare cabin before I go.'

Max laughed.

'Thanks, but I was only joking. Mum and Dad complain I'm never home as it is.'

'Well, the offer stands, if you change your mind,' said Captain Boom. He reached up, took a battered tin from a cupboard on the wall and shook its contents out.

Max gaped at the tangle of jewellery, coins and notes that spilled over the work surface.

'How do you want to be paid? Jewellery or cash?' asked Captain Boom.

'Cash, please,' said Max quickly. 'I'm saving up for a new bike, and the shop only takes money.'

'Not very adventurous of it,' said Captain Boom.

'Tell me about it.' Max sighed. 'It does part exchange, but the man wouldn't even consider swapping my sister for the bike I want.'

Captain Boom laughed.

'I tried swapping Treasure once for Becky's third-best cannon. When Becky discovered Treasure was my sister she tied me to the mast and used me as a target to practise her knife-throwing trick.' Captain Boom shuddered. 'You don't mess with Captain Becky Bones!'

As Max left the *Leaky Dip* Becky Bones was sat on her deck peeling an orange with a sword. Seeing Max watching her, she suddenly threw the orange into the air. The sword flashed, then orange segments rained from the sky. Deftly Becky caught the pieces on the sword's blade and popped each one into her mouth.

'Phew,' said Max, hopping on to his bike and pedalling out of the marina. 'I'd rather arm-wrestle with an octopus than upset her!'

CHAPTER FOUR

A CRY FOR HELP

Max couldn't wait to start his new pet-sitting job. The following morning, before breakfast, he went on the Internet to look for information on parrots.

'Parrots are noisy, sociable birds. They are quick to learn and are good mimics,' Max read. 'Pet parrots need challenging toys to stop them from getting bored. Climbing is a favourite pastime. They mustn't be left alone with furniture or electrical wires as they might damage them.'

There were lots of pictures of parrot toys, some of which reminded Max of the toys he'd had as a baby. Mum had kept all the favourite ones and, turning out the cupboard under the stairs, Max found his old wooden shape sorter.

'Squawk will love this,' he said, wiping off the dust.

'What've you got there?' asked Alice, sneaking up behind him. 'Ooooh, do you need help, little Max? Can't you work out which shape goes through which hole?'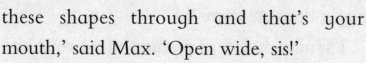

'There's only one hole big enough to fit these shapes through and that's your mouth,' said Max. 'Open wide, sis!'

'Hmph' snorted Alice. 'You're the one

with the big mouth. Watch what you say, Max, cos one day that mouth is going to get you into BIG trouble!'

'You wish!' said Max, slipping past Alice and going to put the shape sorter in a carrier bag, ready to take with him when he left to visit Squawk.

It was still early when Max arrived at the marina. No one was about as he chained his bike to a mooring ring. With the carrier bag in one hand Max stepped onto the *Leaky Dip*'s gangplank. If anything, the gangplank was even more wonky than it had been the day before.

'Captain Boom kept his promise to fix it then . . . not!' muttered Max.

'STOP!'

It was the same fierce voice that Max

had heard the day before, and once again he froze.

'Put your hands in the air.'

'What? No way. Look, I . . .'

BANG . . . WHOOOO . . . SPLASH!

Max never saw the cannonball, but it sounded very close and he immediately raised his hands above his head.

'That was just a warning,' said the scary voice. 'The next ball's got your name on it. So let's try again. Hands in the air and walk forward nice and slow.'

Slow as a sloth, Max inched his way along the gangplank until the voice called out again, 'Good. Now hop.'

'But—' squeaked Max.

'HOP!' roared the voice.

Max hopped, and his heart hopped too each time his foot left the rickety gangplank. Would he make it, or would he end up falling in the sea? Six agonizing hops later and Max was safely aboard the *Leaky Dip*. He risked a quick look round, but the deck was empty.

'STAND STILL!' roared the voice suddenly. 'What's in the bag?'

'A toy,' said Max, pulling out the shape sorter. 'It's for Squawk to play with. Squawk's a parrot. I'm—'

'I know who Squawk is! Squawk doesn't like toys for babies and nor do I. Next time bring sweets.'

'Sweets?' repeated Max in surprise.

'Jelly babies,' said the voice. 'So I can pull their heads off. Bring me jelly babies tomorrow or I'll pull your head off instead. Got that? Good. Now hop it.'

Max stared around but he could see no sign of the speaker. Was it safe to stay on the boat, or should he leave?

I've got to stay, Max decided. I can't leave Squawk here on his own.

Nervously Max crossed the main deck to the small aviary Captain Boom had shown him yesterday. Although Squawk was uncaged by day, Captain Boom insisted on locking him up at night.

'People steal parrots,' he'd told Max. 'They're worth a lot of money.'

Squawk was still asleep. Head tucked under one multicoloured wing, he was snoring loudly.

Max chuckled. He'd never heard of a snoring parrot.

'Squawk,' he called softly, 'wake up. It's Max. Your pet sitter.'

Squawk woke so quickly that Max suspected he hadn't been asleep at all. He wondered if Squawk had heard the strange voice and seen Max hopping up the gangplank. It was an embarrassing thought.

'Time for breakfast,' said Max, unlocking the aviary. 'It's mango this morning.'

'Hello, Mat,' said Squawk. 'Hello, door-mat.'

Max was thinking up a smart reply when a childlike cry made him spin round.

'Help!'

It sounded like a little girl, and it was coming from the top of the mast.

'Help!'

Screwing up his eyes against the morning sun, Max scanned the mast, but he couldn't see anyone there.

'Where are you?' he called.

'Up here.'

'Where? I can't see you.'

'I'm in the crow's nest.'

Max stared up to the special lookout post at the top of the mast. It was empty. The little girl must be very tiny if he couldn't see her over the top of its sides.

'Who are you? What are you doing up there?' shouted Max.

'I got lost. I thought if I climbed up high I might be able to see where I was going.'

'Come down,' said Max. 'Come down slowly and I'll help you find your way home.'

'I can't!' The voice rose to a squeal. 'I'm stuck! I'm too scared to move!'

'Ooooh!' Squawk stepped out of the aviary and waddled towards Max. 'Sounds like a job for me. I'll fly up and help her down, shall I?'

'Ha! So you *can* talk properly!' exclaimed Max. 'I knew it!'

Max was used to pet-sitting for talking animals, and Captain Boom had said that Squawk was a chatterbox.

'Course I can talk, bilge bucket! You

humans! You're all the same. You think you're the only ones born with a tongue!'

'Help!' called the little girl. 'I'm going to fall.'

'Quick! I'll go,' Squawk flapped his feathers as he prepared to take off.

'No!' said Max. 'You're not allowed up the mast. I'll go.'

'Spoilsport,' said Squawk. 'Well, don't go shouting for help when you get stuck too!'

'I won't,' said Max. 'I'm good at climbing.'

The mast was higher than it looked. Max climbed as fast as he dared while calling comforting words to the little girl, who was now crying. Reaching the crow's nest, Max sighed with relief. He'd made it! He raised his head over the top of the platform, kicked his legs and arrived in a heap. Quickly sitting up, Max stared round in surprise. The crow's nest was empty.

'Hello?' shouted
Max. 'Where are you?'

'Down here.' The
little girl dissolved
into giggles.

Crossly Max looked down at the deck. It was like peering the wrong way through a telescope. Everything was in miniature! The splash of red, yellow and blue was Squawk. That dirty white bundle was a pile of old sails, the brown snake was a rope, and Max could even see a broken oar. But there was no sign of the little girl!

'Where down there?' shouted Max, somewhat irritated.

'Here . . . And here . . . And here . . . Over here . . . I'm here!'

The little girl's voice seemed to come at

Max from all directions. It echoed from down on the deck right up to the Jolly Roger at the very top of the mast. For a second Max wondered if he was losing the plot, then suddenly he got it! He'd been had! The voices and noises weren't real. None of them. Not the cannon fire, nor the scary voice that had forced him to hop up the gangplank. It was all a trick. And if he wasn't mistaken, Squawk was to blame.

'Parrots are good mimics,' Max remembered. 'And very good at throwing their voices too, by the sound of it!' he muttered.

Max started to laugh. 'Blazing beaks!' he exclaimed. 'I've been tricked by a parrot!'

CHAPTER FIVE
UPSETTING BECKY BONES

Max then heard Squawk's raucous cries of laughter. The parrot probably thought him a right nerdy-no-brain, falling for his tricks so easily!

Max gazed around, determined to make the most of the view before he climbed back down to the deck. He could see why Squawk liked playing on the mast. It was brilliant being so high up. It was also a great place for spying. Max could clearly see the *Leaky Dip*'s neighbour, the *Shark's Teeth*, and even in miniature she was a boat to admire.

'I'd love a ride on her,' said Max wistfully. 'I bet she's really fast.'

Max loved fast things. Unfortunately his parents didn't. Mum was the worst. She drove so slowly that even tractors overtook her! On board the *Shark's Teeth* a door burst open and Captain Becky Bones came running up on deck.

'Ahoy there, *Leaky Dip*,' she bellowed. 'Cut the noise. I'm trying to listen to the shipping news!'

Max chuckled softly as Squawk immediately stopped laughing. Then, to his horror, his own voice shouted back at Becky:

'Ahoy there, *Shark's Teeth*. Get a life. Listen to the Music Channel instead!'

Max whipped around, almost expecting to see his double sat behind him in the

230

crow's nest. But of course there was nobody there. The voice had come from Squawk. He was mimicking Max and throwing his voice up to the top of the mast so it sounded like Max was doing the talking!

'What did you say?' Becky shook her fist skywards. 'Say that again and I'll have you for fish bait.'

'It wasn't me,' said Max, but his words were drowned out by his own voice calling, 'Fish bait yourself! You smell like it!'

'Squawk, stop it!'

Max had to shut Squawk up. Frantically he slithered down the mast. His legs snagged in the rigging and he got a splinter

in his hand, but he didn't dare stop. Soon he was low enough to jump. He landed heavily, biting his tongue. Ignoring the pain, he hurtled across the main deck and threw himself at Squawk.

Squawk had been enjoying himself so much that he didn't see Max coming for him. 'Guuuuurrr, get off.'

'No way,' said Max, clamping Squawk's beak shut.

'Get off or I'll ring Parrotline,' mumbled Squawk. 'I know my rights.'

'What about *my* rights?' growled Max. 'My right not to end up as fish food.'

Keeping one hand firmly on Squawk's beak, Max called an apology to Becky Bones, then bundled Squawk below deck and into the galley.

'Like apologizing will help,' said Squawk smugly when Max let him go. 'Becky'll think you're a looney tune. Insulting her one minute, then apologizing the next. That was soooo funny! I'm a good mimic, aren't I?'

Max felt his lips twitch but he made them stay in a frown.

Squawk rubbed his head against Max's hand.

'I didn't mean to get you into trouble. I just got carried away.'

'Is that an apology?' asked Max.

'Yes,' said Squawk. 'Am I forgiven?'

'Only if you promise not to pull a stunt like that again,' said Max sternly. Then, unable to help himself, he burst into laughter.

Squawk laughed too, rolling on to his back and kicking his claws in the air until Max tickled his tummy. Then he righted himself fast!

'You can make it up to me by teaching me how to throw my voice,' Max suggested. I could use that trick at school! But now I'm going to cut up the mango Captain Boom left for your breakfast.'

'Bring me jelly babies tomorrow or I'll

pull your head off,' Squawk growled in the same fierce voice he'd used earlier.

'No more tricks,' said Max, slicing into the mango. 'Do you hear me?'

'No more tricks and that's a promise,' agreed Squawk, saluting Max with one wing.

CHAPTER SIX
AN ACCIDENT

The first day spent pet-sitting for Squawk was fun but exhausting! Max really liked the cheeky parrot, but he was very lively and barely stopped talking, even to breathe! Squawk didn't play any more tricks. Instead he taught Max how to project his voice, and by the end of the day Max was quite good at it.

'Bedtime, Squawk,' said Max. His voice sounded like it came from the rusty cannon.

'You're not going to lock me up, are you?' asked Squawk, swallowing his last piece of honey-coated toast.

'I am,' said Max.

'Why? I promise I'll be good. I won't go up the mast. I'll go and sleep in my tree.'

Squawk cocked his head and made sad eyes at Max.

'Don't!' exclaimed Max, feeling guilty. 'I have to lock you up. Captain Boom's worried you might get stolen.'

'Stolen!'

'Yeah!' Max chuckled. 'Anyone who stole you would soon bring you back! But that's not the point. I promised Captain Boom that I'd lock you up at night.'

'Like he keeps his promises,' said Squawk. 'His favourite saying is "That's a promise", but he never keeps any of them.'

'Oh,' exclaimed Max. 'So that's why he

didn't fix the gangplank!'

'S'right,' said Squawk. 'Captain Boom keeps promising to take me for a ride on a real boat – one that doesn't leak. But he hasn't done that yet either!'

'I'm sure he will,' soothed Max. 'Now please get into your aviary. It's bedtime, and I've got to go home for tea.'

Squawk waddled across the deck in his ungainly style, but stopped at the aviary door.

'Don't bother locking it,' he said. 'I can get out.'

'How?' asked Max.

Squawk tapped his beak with a wing.

'Like I'd tell you.'

'Promise me you won't do anything silly,' said Max.

'Like you care!'

'I do actually,' said Max. 'But then I've always had a soft spot for nutters!'

'Very funny, I'm sure' said Squawk, flapping into the aviary. 'Watch out, Max! I'll get you for that!'

'In your dreams,' said Max, padlocking the aviary door. 'And I hope they're sweet ones. Night, Squawk. See you tomorrow.'

Max slept so deeply he didn't hear his alarm ringing. The sun woke him, squeezing through a chink in the curtains. Leaping out of bed, Max pulled on his clothes.

'Squawk is not going to be happy with me,' he panted as he raced for the bathroom.

Alice was in there, and no amount of banging on the door would shift her. Max gave up on a wash, waved a comb at his unruly hair, grabbed a piece of toast from the rack on the table and bolted out to the shed to get his bike. He pedalled to the marina so fast his tyres almost smoked. He didn't slow down until he'd chained his bike to the *Leaky Dip*'s mooring ring and was halfway up the gangplank. Then he stopped dead. The gangplank was wobbling ominously.

'Not so fast,' he told himself.

Slowly Max took one step. The gangplank groaned. Max waited for it to settle, then took another careful step. This time the gangplank juddered then suddenly plunged into the water, tipping Max in too. 'Urrrgh!' Max gasped in surprise.

He trod water for a moment to get his bearings. He was halfway between the

Leaky Dip and the shore. Max was deciding which way to swim when the gangplank floated up behind him and bopped him on the head. He spluttered, sank under the water and when he surfaced a long strand of seaweed was stuck to his face. Max thought he heard a giggle, but he was too busy trying to stay afloat to wonder about it. His clothes and trainers were full of water, and the extra weight was pulling him down.

Panting like a dog, Max struck out for the *Leaky Dip*. But he hadn't realized how high the boat's deck was above the sea's surface. He couldn't quite reach it, and with each failed attempt he swallowed another mouthful of salty water.

'Hang on!' called a voice.

Max heard something whizzing through the air, then felt another blow to the back of his head. It pushed him under and when he surfaced again, coughing up more water, he found his arms were pinned to his sides.

'Argh!' Max yelped.

He struggled fiercely until he realized he was fighting with a life ring. Wriggling like a caterpillar, he squeezed first one arm and then the other over the top of the ring.

'Hurray!'

From the handrail of the *Leaky Dip* Squawk cheered wildly.

'Squawk! How did . . . ?' Max broke off, suddenly realizing that the current was pulling him towards the *Shark's Teeth*.

CHAPTER SEVEN

A PROPER PROMISE

'**E**r, morning,' Max called out politely.

Becky Bones was only little, but her loud voice made up for her slight frame.

'What do you think you're playing at?' she bellowed.

'Erm, I'm having a wash,' said Max, splashing water over his face. 'I'm running late this morning, there was a queue for the bathroom—'

'This is a marina,' Becky cut in angrily, 'not a hotel. I'm trying to practise my sword dance and you're distracting me. I nearly chopped my toe off just then. Come any closer and I'll make you walk the plank.'

'Nice to meet you too,' muttered Max, frantically kicking his skinny legs against the current as he fought his way back to the *Leaky Dip*.

'Go, Max,' yelled Squawk excitedly.

The parrot moved down and began pulling at something on the deck. Suddenly a bundle of rope slithered over the side and into the water.

'Yo!' screeched Squawk as the rope ladder unfolded.

Gratefully Max reached out and climbed aboard the *Leaky Dip*. Water gushed from him, and a shell fell out of his trainers when he pulled them off.

Squawk hopped up and

down the handrail screeching with laughter.

'That was a good one!' he shouted. 'That was my best ever.'

'What do you mean?' asked Max coldly. 'And how did you get out of your aviary?'

'Told you I could!' Squawk stopped laughing and looked smug. 'It's easy. I picked the lock. But I didn't expect you to fall in. That was wild!'

'What do you mean?'

'The gangplank joke. It wasn't meant to fall in the water. Just slip a little to give you a fright.'

'You set me up? But you promised there'd be no more tricks.'

'We don't keep promises on the *Leaky Dip*,' said Squawk.

'Well, it's about time you did, shrimp face!' spluttered Max. 'You could have drowned me.'

'Keep your feathers on,' said Squawk calmly. 'You sound like Becky Bones. It was a joke. No harm done.'

'No harm done?! Look at me,' said Max.

'So you're a bit wet! What's the big deal? You can borrow something to change into. Captain Boom's got tons of clothes,'

'That's OK then,' said Max sarcastically, 'cos we're easily the same size, aren't we?'

Squawk's face fell. 'Oooh, I didn't think of that. Never mind. You'll soon dry in the sun, and there's a good sea breeze.'

Max glared at Squawk, thinking of all the horrible things he'd like to do to the parrot to get his own back. Then he heard his own voice repeating:

'I'm having a wash. I'm running late this morning, there was a queue for the bathroom.'

Then Becky's rougher tones answered,

'This is a marina, not a hotel.'

Squawk was so good at mimicking Becky that Max couldn't help but laugh. And once he'd started laughing he saw the funny side of Squawk's joke and he laughed even more. Squawk joined in. He lay on his back and, kicking his claws in the air, laughed hysterically. Max tried that too, kicking his legs in the air, until, remembering his pet-

sitting duties, he sat up.

'I'll go and get your breakfast. I think it's oats with linseed oil and kiwi fruit today.'

'Yum, yum,' said Squawk. 'I'll just sit here in the sun and let you wait on me then.'

'Fine,' said Max. 'But no more tricks, OK?'

'I promise,' said Squawk.

'A proper promise, not a *Leaky Dip* one?'

'A proper promise,' agreed Squawk. 'Don't be long. I'm starving!'

Max squelched down to the galley to prepare Squawk's breakfast. He peeled and sliced the kiwi fruit, then arranged it over the oats. Next he drizzled linseed oil on top. Pleased with his efforts, Max carried the dish of food back on deck to Squawk.

'Yummy,' said Squawk, swiping a piece of kiwi fruit before Max had even put the dish down. 'I'm starving.'

'Slow down,' laughed Max. 'You'll make yourself sick.'

While Squawk gobbled his breakfast Max tidied up the aviary. Then he nipped down to the galley to refill Squawk's bowl of water.

As Max stepped back on deck the *Leaky Dip* rolled suddenly. Max wobbled, almost spilling the water. Carefully he made his way back to the aviary. The wind was getting up, and Max's wet clothes flapped uncomfortably. Someone was shouting. It sounded like Becky Bones. Max grinned, glad he wasn't getting a telling-off this time. The shouting grew louder. Then there was a tremendous *bang!* The *Leaky Dip* shuddered so violently that Max fell head first into the aviary and dropped the water bowl on his toe.

'Ouch!' he yelled, shaking his wet foot. 'Squawk, what are you doing now?'

It sounded like the parrot was messing about with the old cannon. Max legged it back to the main deck but Squawk was no where near the cannon. He was staring at the *Shark's Teeth*. On board, Captain Becky Bones was leaping in the air.

'Come back here,' howled Becky, waving her sword at Max.

'Yeah, right,' whispered Max. 'So you can cut us up and feed us to the fish. I don't think so. What's she cross about this time?'

'Can't you guess?' Squawk's tiny eyes were bright with fear and Max realized he was missing something.

'Guess what?'

'We just crashed into the *Shark's Teeth* and put a dent in the side.'

'What? How could we?'

'Because no one's steering the boat,' said Squawk.

'What are you talking about? You don't steer a boat that's tied up in a marina.'

'But we're not,' whispered Squawk. 'We've come adrift. We're heading out to sea.'

CHAPTER EIGHT

SQUAWK AT SEA

Squawk hung his head.

'It was an accident,' he mumbled. 'I think I untied the wrong rope when I was setting up the gangplank trick.'

'Great,' said Max. 'I feel much better now I know you didn't mean to do it.'

'Really?'

'No,' said Max. 'Remind me – where is the ship's wheel?'

'Over there,' said Squawk, pointing a multicoloured wing at a large wooden wheel on the main deck. 'But . . .'

As Max ran to the ship's wheel he tried to

remember how to steer a boat. He'd done it once before, on holiday. It wasn't like steering a bicycle or a car. You had to turn the wheel and wait for the wind to take you where you wanted to go. The *Leaky Dip*'s wheel was as battered as the rest of the ship. Carefully Max grasped it between his skinny hands and turned it to the left. Nothing happened. Perhaps it took even longer to turn this type of boat?

Max hung on, willing the boat to turn. When it didn't, he spun the wheel round further.

'It doesn't work very well,' said

Squawk, flying over. 'It's broken. Captain Boom's never bothered to fix it because the *Leaky Dip* has too many holes to go sailing in her.'

'Have you got *any* good news?' snapped Max.

'Er, I don't expect we'll get that far. Not without a sail.'

'We've drifted quite a way already,' said Max, looking back at the marina. 'The current's pulling us. We're going to have to put the sail up or we'll never get back. We'll just drift further out.'

Squawk brightened. 'Does that mean I get to go up the mast?'

Max did some quick thinking. He couldn't be in two places at once, and it would probably be safer to let Squawk put the sail up than let him steer the boat. The wheel was heavy, and Max doubted Squawk would be able to turn it.

'OK, but no tricks. You put the sail up and come straight back. This is serious, Squawk. We could drown if you mess around.'

Squawk looked offended.

'I'm not an airhead,' he said gruffly.

'No, you're a birdbrain,' chuckled Max. 'Now go and get that sail up. We're almost out on the open sea.'

Enthusiastically Squawk flew off to unfurl the mainsail. Max, a hand shielding his green eyes from the sun, watched as the bird untied each of the ropes that bound the sail to the mast. But his relief was short-lived. As the sail began to unfold, Max saw it was full of holes. When Squawk finally returned to the deck Max couldn't help commenting, 'It's more string vest than sail.'

Squawk groaned, then tucked his head under his wing.

'It wasn't that funny,' said Max.

'Not laughing,' moaned Squawk. 'I don't feel well. I feel sick.'

'You probably ate your breakfast too fast,' said Max, unsympathetically.

'I always eat that fast,' said Squawk. 'This is different. I feel awful. Stop the boat from going up and down!'

'So sorry, I'll try and find a flat bit of sea!'

Experimentally Max wiggled the ship's wheel.

'No, can't find any flat bits. It's got something to do with these pesky waves!' he said with even more sarcasm.

'I'm going to be . . .' Squawk lurched forward and was sick all over Max's shoe.

'*Gross!*' thought Max, then, remembering he was the pet sitter, he pulled a very damp tissue from his pocket and carefully wiped Squawk's beak.

'Better now?'

'Noooooo,' moaned Squawk. 'Not better. I want to go back. Don't like it out here. The sea's too wonky.'

'You get seasick?' Max was incredulous. 'Whoever heard of a pirate's parrot suffering from seasickness?'

'Runs in the family,' Squawk whimpered. 'My uncle ran away with a circus cos the sea makes him so ill.'

'Do you want to go and sit in your tree? I'll carry you there if you like.'

'Noooo,' groaned Squawk. 'I want to lie down.'

'Shall I make you a bed then?'

'Yes, please.'

Max looked at the junk around him. There was plenty here to make Squawk a comfortable bed. With one hand still on the ship's wheel Max stretched out and managed to pull a battered old crate towards him. Then, hooking a piece of sailcloth over his foot, he lifted that over too. The sailcloth fitted perfectly inside the crate. Max quickly let go of the ship's wheel to help Squawk into his new bed.

'Is that better?'

'Yes,' said Squawk, 'but I wouldn't mind a drink of water.'

Max looked around. They'd safely passed all the boats in the marina and had almost reached the open sea. Max knew a little about wind and how it affected the direction a boat could take. Once out at sea Max hoped to sail the *Leaky Dip* in a circle to bring her back to the marina. At the speed they were travelling, he probably had enough time to nip down to the galley and get Squawk some water before he made the turn.

'I'll be one second,' he said.

Faster than a galleon in a gale Max raced to the galley. He filled a bowl with water, then rushed back to find Squawk had fallen asleep.

'Great,' said Max. He was thirsty himself now, but he didn't dare leave the ship's wheel again. The *Leaky Dip* was already drifting away to the left. Max fixed his eye on a red buoy and steered towards it. At first the boat didn't seem to respond, but after a while Max was happy they were travelling in the direction he wanted to go. Enviously he watched a sleek boat coming up fast behind the *Leaky Dip*. The boat had three masts, each with a pennant flying from the top. Max squinted at the pennants, trying to work out what was on them. A sudden boom made him jump. Something whistled through the air and splashed into the sea a short way from the *Leaky Dip*.

'Snapping sharks!' exclaimed Max.

Now the boat was closer he could clearly see its three pennants. Each had a skull and crossbones, with red blood oozing from the eye sockets.

There was another bang and Max ducked as a cannonball hurtled from  one of the six gleaming cannons on board. Amazingly the cannonball splashed into the sea, missing the *Leaky Dip* by a shrimp's leg.

'Oh no!' groaned Max, a cold feeling

stealing over him. 'It's the *Shark's Teeth*, and I don't think Becky Bones is trying to invite me to lunch.'

CHAPTER NINE
THE BATTLE

The noise woke Squawk. Woozily he sat up and was sick over Max's other shoe.

'Nice,' sighed Max. 'A matching pair!'

'Water,' quavered Squawk. 'I need a drink.'

Max quickly let go of the ship's wheel to push Squawk's water bowl closer. The parrot took a few sips, then leaned against Max's leg.

'How are you feeling now?' he asked.

'Sick as a parrot,' moaned Squawk.

Max stroked the parrot's head. He didn't like seeing him in this state. He preferred

Squawk the joker.

'We'll soon be home,' he said, sneakily glancing back at the *Shark's Teeth*.

The rival boat was approaching fast. Max could see Captain Becky Bones furiously waving her sword at the *Leaky Dip*. She shouted something that Max couldn't hear. Max willed the *Leaky Dip* on, but if anything she seemed to be slowing down. Max knew his only chance was to get back to the marina. It should be busy there by now. Too busy for Captain Bones to carry out her worst threats. But out here on the open sea Max could be made to walk the plank and only the fish would know! Were there sharks this close to the shore? Max shivered. He didn't know and he didn't want to find out!

'Squawk,' said Max casually, 'where does Captain Boom keep his cannonballs?'

'Under his bunk,' said Squawk. 'Why?'

'Erm,' Max hesitated, not sure how much to tell Squawk when he was so unwell.

'Becky Bones is after us, isn't she?'

Max laughed. Squawk was too clever for his own good!

'Yes.'

'S'good, said Squawk, closing his eyes. 'She'll soon put me out of my misery!'

'That's not going to happen,' said Max. 'We'll be back in the marina soon, and then you'll feel better.'

He glanced at the *Shark's Teeth* again. The boat was definitely gaining on the *Leaky Dip*. Max didn't have any option. He would have to leave the wheel in order to fetch a supply of cannonballs. Gently he lifted Squawk back into his makeshift bed.

'Stay there,' he said.

'Like I'm going anywhere else,' muttered the parrot.

Once again Max raced below deck. Captain Boom's cabin was easily the messiest place on board ship. Max waded through dirty clothes, towels and a mountain of *Pirate Weekly* magazines until he reached the bunk. He scrabbled around underneath it, pulling out more junk until he found what he was looking for. A rusty iron ball a bit smaller than a football.

'Is that it?' muttered Max, feeling under the bunk again. 'There must be more than one.'

But there wasn't. Disappointed, Max

carried the cannonball back on deck. The *Shark's Teeth* was much closer now. The moment Max took hold of the *Leaky Dip*'s wheel Becky Bones started shouting at him again. Max closed his ears and concentrated on steering the boat back towards the harbour.

They were making very slow progress. The *Leaky Dip* groaned and leaned sharply to the right. Max hung on to the wheel and used his foot to stop Squawk's bed from sliding away. Then Max noticed the water. The deck was like a paddling pool. Max, whose trainers were still wet after his early-morning swim, was shocked that he hadn't noticed the flooded deck before.

'Snapping sharks!' he exclaimed. 'We're sinking.'

'Man the lifeboat,' said Squawk weakly.

Max brightened.

'Good idea. Where is it?'

'There isn't one. Captain Boom keeps promising to buy one, but . . .' Squawk shrugged his wings.

'Another *Leaky Dip* promise,' sighed Max.

As fast as the *Leaky Dip* was filling up with water, so the *Shark's Teeth* was getting closer. Max gave up trying to steer while he prepared the cannon.

'We're going down fighting,' he said.

'Matches in the locker over there,' said Squawk.

Luckily the water hadn't reached the locker. Pocketing the matches, Max loaded the cannonball and took aim. The *Shark's Teeth* drew alongside the *Leaky Dip*. Max heard scrabbling, like an enormous rat, then Captain Becky Bones climbed up over the handrail, a rope in her mouth.

'Hold your fire,' she said with her mouth full.

'Yeah, right!' muttered Max, lighting the match.

There was a muffled bang, followed by a small thud. A thick cloud of black dust burst from the end of the cannon. Then the cannon ball plopped out and rolled across the *Leaky Dip*'s wet deck. Max coughed and wiped the dust from his eyes. Typical! Even the cannon didn't work properly.

'I should have guessed,' groaned Max, wishing he'd thought to arm himself. Even a frying pan would have been better than nothing. But it was too late now.

'Shiver me shoes!' roared Captain Becky Bones, leaping aboard. 'What part of hold your fire didn't you understand?'

Deftly she tied the *Shark's Teeth*'s mooring rope to a ring on deck, then, spitting on her hand, she rubbed at her sooty face.

'I don't know why I'm bothering to rescue you,' she said fiercely.

Max stared in amazement. He was so scared that his brain was having trouble working everything out.

'Rescue us? But you've just tried to sink us with cannonballs.'

'That was to get your attention. I'd have hit you if I'd wanted to.'

'You've really come to save us?'

'Yes,' growled Becky Bones, as if she hadn't really wanted to. 'Your boat's dangerous. It's too full of holes to sail anywhere.'

'But why would you help us?'

'I owe Captain Boom a favour. When I accidentally cut off my finger, practising sword moves, Captain Boom drove me to hospital, where a clever doctor sewed it back on. See?' Proudly Becky Bones showed Max a wonky finger with a neat scar at its base.

'Captain Boom always seems a little scared of me, but I couldn't let the *Leaky Dip* sink. I might not get such a helpful neighbour next time.'

Max grinned with relief. 'That's lucky.'

'It will be if we make it back. You're not out of the water yet!' Becky Bones laughed at her own joke. 'Better get a move on before I change my mind and leave you to sink!'

CHAPTER TEN
ONE MORE PROMISE

The journey back to the marina was long and slow. Even under tow, Max still had to steer the *Leaky Dip* while baling out the water at the same time. He also had to take care of Squawk. But once they were safely back in their old mooring the sick parrot quickly perked up, until Becky produced a list of chores she wanted doing to make up for the dent in the *Shark's Teeth*.

'Sick as a parrot,' wailed Squawk when Max told him their first job was to scrub the decks.

'You'll be sicker than a parrot if you

don't lend a wing,' said Max sternly. 'I'll lock you in your aviary, and this time I'll use the padlock from my bicycle chain. It's a number combination so you won't be able to pick that!'

'Huh! You're harder than Becky's Bones!' joked Squawk.

'What's that about my bones?'

Squawk jumped guiltily, but there was no one there.

'What . . . ?'

Max grinned.

'Get a move on bird brain,' he said in Becky's gruff voice.

Squawk laughed.

'Nice one, Max. You had me fooled.'

'Good,' said Max. 'But no more jokes. It's time to work.'

Squawk and
Max sat on a branch
in Squawk's tree,
watching for Captain
Boom, who was due
home any minute.

'There he is,' shouted
Squawk excitedly as a
battered car pulled up
next to the *Leaky Dip*'s
gangplank. 'Last one
down's a dodo.'

Squawk launched himself
from the branch and flew

towards the gangplank. Max slithered down the tree trunk. He was miles behind Squawk, but still in time to see Captain Boom stumble on the wonky gangplank and almost fall into the sea.

'I'll fix that today, and that's a promise,' puffed Captain Boom as he stepped on deck. 'Hello, you two. How did it go?'

'Good, thanks,' said Max. 'How was Treasure?'

'Same as usual. How was Squawk?'

'He was good.'

'Really?!' Captain Boom sounded surprised. 'What – no tricks, no jokes? He didn't upset Captain Becky Bones even once?'

'Erm, Squawk was Squawk,' said Max, truthfully.

Captain Boom stared at Squawk, and Squawk stared innocently back.

'So you'd look after him again?'

'Yes, I'd definitely pet-sit for you again.'
Max winked at Squawk. 'And that's a promise!'

Me and Squawk

For Daniel and Jamie – J.S.
For Joseph – N.R.

CONTENTS

CHAPTER ONE
SEAGULL TOWERS

The phone was ringing. Max dashed out of his bedroom, raced down the stairs and snatched it up.

'Hello,' he said. 'This is Max the Pet Sitter.'

'Hello, Max,' said a cheery voice. 'This is Ned Nettles the Pet Owner. Can you pet-sit for me? I'm going away for a week to help my sister out. She runs a youth club and one of her staff is sick.'

'Sure,' said Max. 'What sort of pet have you got?'

'A puppy,' said Ned. 'He's adorable.

Why not come over and meet him? I live at Flat 6, Seagull Towers.'

'I'm on my way,' said Max, and put the phone down.

Max wrote Ned's address in his pet sitter's notebook, then hurried out to the garden to get his bike from the shed. Mum was weeding the rose bed.

'Going somewhere?' she asked, waving the trowel at him.

'Seagull Towers, to meet a puppy and a man called Ned Nettles.'

'That'll be fun,' said Mum. 'You've always wanted a puppy.'

It was true. Max desperately wanted a pet of his own, but he couldn't have one because his annoying big sister, Alice, was allergic to animals. As Max cycled to Seagull Towers he wondered what the puppy would be like. Ned Nettles had called his pet adorable, and Max imagined a cute little animal with floppy ears and big brown eyes. Ned sounded nice too. Max decided he would be young and friendly with a smiley face.

It wasn't far to Seagull Towers. Max pedalled up the drive and stopped in surprise by a large sign.

'Seagull Towers,' he read. 'No Skate-boards. No Ball Games. No Pets. By Order of the Caretaker.'

That couldn't be right! Max pulled his pet sitter's notebook out of his pocket to check he had the right address.

He was flicking through the pages when a voice called out, 'Hello, are you Max?'

Max looked up. Seagull Towers was a huge old house with three floors and two turrets. A very grand stone staircase led up to an enormous revolving front door, and standing at the top of it was a wrinkled old man with spiky silver hair.

'Max?' he called again, and when Max nodded the man swung a leg over the stone handrail and slid down the banister.

'Ned Nettles,' he said, landing almost on Max's toes. 'Thanks for coming so quickly.'

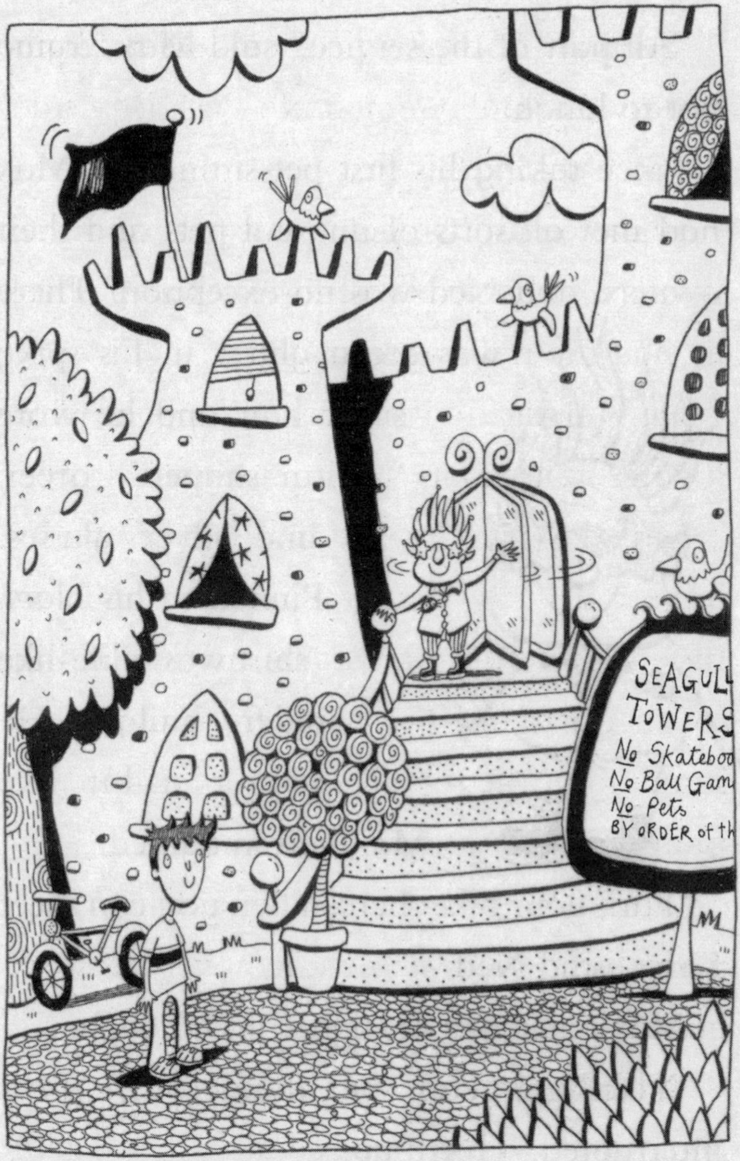
SEAGULL
TOWERS
No Skatebo
No Ball Gam
No Pets
BY ORDER of th

'All part of the service,' said Max, trying not to laugh.

Since taking his first pet-sitting job Max had met all sorts of unusual pets and their owners, and Ned was no exception! There was green glitter in his spiky silver hair and he wore star-shaped green and silver glasses. Pinned to his black shirt was a life-like spider badge. He wasn't a bit like Max had imagined.

'Park your bike there. Then you can meet Fang,' said Ned.

Max pointed at the sign. 'But I thought . . .'

'Thinking can be dangerous,' Ned interrupted. 'Hurry up.'

As Max chained his bike to the signpost something hit him in the back of the legs.

'Oomph!' he spluttered, almost head-butting his back wheel. He spun round.

'Woo, woo, wooooo!' panted an untidy bundle of grey fur. 'Woo, woo, wooooo!'

'Nice dog,' said Max, hesitantly putting out a hand, then pulling it back again when he saw the size of Fang's teeth.

'Quiet, Fang,' hissed Ned, and then, 'Fang, that's naughty.'

Fang was attacking the signpost. Ned pulled him away, then prized a long splinter of wood from the puppy's mouth.

'How many times have I told you not to chew?' he said, pretending to be cross.

Max gasped. Fang's teeth must be really sharp to do that amount of damage. He hoped the puppy was going to be friendly. It would be awful if Fang decided to take a chunk out of him!

'Fang, say hello to Max.'

Ned let the puppy go again.

'Woooooo, woo, woo, wooooo!' squealed Fang, rushing back to Max.

Fang had wolf-like blue eyes, a long snout and wicked claws. Max tensed as Fang jumped towards him, but the puppy only wanted to lick him. Max laughed, patting the bits of the leaping Fang he could reach, until he realized he was standing in a puddle.

'Whoops! Someone's had an accident.' Max lifted a sodden trainer.

'That's no accident.' Ned grinned. 'It's a compliment. Fang's excited. He only does that when he really likes someone.'

'Nice!' said Max. 'So what does he do to people he doesn't like?'

Ned tapped the side of his nose. 'Best not ask,' he said.

CHAPTER TWO
A SECRET

'Come and see my flat,' said Ned once Fang had calmed down.

He hurried up the stone staircase and Max had to run to catch him as he disappeared through the revolving door. Max followed, and the door whisked him round and spat him out so quickly that he landed on his bottom in the reception hall. A large woman with a chin as bristly as a porcupine peered over the counter.

'Morning, Ned, and who's that?'

Ned hauled Max to his feet.

'This is Max the Plant Sitter. He's going

to water my plants for me while I'm away. Max, meet Bertha Crab, our caretaker.'

Max opened his mouth to correct Ned, then shut it again in surprise as Ned slyly kicked his ankle. He looked around for Fang, but the puppy seemed to have disappeared.

'Hello, Bertha,' said Max.

'It's Mrs Crab to you,' sniffed the

caretaker, glaring at Max. 'I hope you're going to behave yourself. The rules are clearly—'

'Yes, yes,' interrupted Ned impatiently. 'Thank you, Bertha, but we've got to dash. Come along, Max.'

Ned's flat was in one of the turrets. He led the way up a spiral staircase to a corridor on the first floor and stopped at a door numbered six.

'Here we are.'

Deftly Ned unpinned his spider badge and threw it at the door. A long silver thread, attached to a tiny cobweb on Ned's shirt, followed the spider. When it hit the door the spider scuttled up to the lock, stuck one leg inside the keyhole and wiggled it. The door opened.

Max gawped, then jumped as Fang suddenly appeared by his feet.

'Where did you get to?' he asked as the puppy barged past him.

'Fang is very good at being invisible,' chuckled Ned. He popped the spider back on his shirt. 'In you go, Max.'

Max stepped inside Ned's flat, curiously peeping into the rooms as Ned led the way to the kitchen. In the lounge stars dangled from the ceiling, and in the bedroom there was everything from a cauldron to a pointed green hat.

'Why did you tell Mrs Crab I'm a Plant Sitter?' he asked.

'Haven't you worked it out yet?' Ned stopped and shook his head. 'And I thought you were clever!'

'You said that thinking can be dangerous,' Max reminded him.

Ned roared with laughter. 'True, but I need some excitement, living here. There are far too many silly rules. No skateboards, no ball games, NO PETS. No fun, if you ask me.'

'Sounds about as interesting as watching a cauldron rust,' Max agreed.

'It was!' said Ned. 'Until I found Fang. Someone left him on the beach, tied up in a sack, with the tide coming in. How could they! Fang's the most adorable werepup in the world.'

'A werepup?!' exclaimed Max. 'Wicked.'

'Wicked he is too,' Ned agreed. 'Spider's teeth, Fang has livened things up! I've had to keep Fang a secret because of the silly no-pets rule, but I've had him for over a week and no one's guessed yet! Not even nosey old Bertha Crab.'

'So, if anyone asks, I'm here to look after your plants.'

'That's right,' said Ned, perching against the kitchen table. 'You mustn't tell anyone about Fang.'

'How do I take him out for walks?' asked Max.

Ned opened a cupboard and brought out an enormous wicker basket with a frilly red cover.

'You have to smuggle

him out of the building in this,' he announced.

Max eyed the basket suspiciously.

'No way! I'll look like Little Red Riding Hood!' he protested.

Ned's cheerful face turned serious.

'Bertha Crab, the caretaker, is even crabbier than her name suggests. If she finds out about Fang, then she'll make him leave, or worse. Bertha used to have a dog, until it chewed her favourite slippers. She was so mad she said the dog was dangerous and made the vet put it to sleep.'

'That's evil!' exclaimed Max.

'I know.' Ned gripped Max's arm. 'That's why you have to promise to keep Fang a secret.'

'I promise,' said Max solemnly. 'I'm good at secrets. I get tons of practice with my sister, Alice. She's got more nose than an aardvark.'

'Good,' said Ned. 'You'll have to be very careful. Bertha Crab is a pain. She's never around when you need her, yet she's sure to turn up like a nasty rash when you don't. And there's one more thing: remember, Fang is a werepup. Never take him out at night. NEVER! There's a full moon soon and anything could happen! Got that? Right, I'll show you what he eats. You'll also need a key and your wages.'

CHAPTER THREE
HOWLING IN THE NIGHT

Max couldn't wait to start pet-sitting Fang. He loved animals, and he loved a challenge, but the first challenge came quicker than he thought. When Max arrived at Seagull Towers the following morning Mrs Crab was waiting for him.

'There was an awful racket last night,' she said, glaring at him over the counter in the reception hall. 'It was coming from Ned's flat and it sounded like an animal.'

Max's stomach turned a somersault. The noise had to be Fang, but why? Max hoped he wasn't hurt.

Mrs Crab stood up.

'I think I'd better come with you and investigate.'

Max did some quick thinking.

'Sorry, Mrs Crab,' he apologized. 'Ned must have left the stereo on. He loves listening to music.'

'Music!' exclaimed Mrs Crab. 'That was music? It sounded like an animal in pain.'

'It was probably opera.' Max fumbled in his pocket for Ned's spare key. 'That's painful to listen to.'

Quickly Max climbed the spiral staircase, then hurried along the corridor. It was very quiet. Too quiet. Max felt slightly sick and wasn't sure whether it was due to the winding staircase or worry. Something fluttered in his hand as he pulled out the spare spider badge Ned had given him. He opened his palm, jumping as the spider leaped for the door.

'What was that?'

Max spun round. Mrs Crab had followed him upstairs.

'Nothing,' he said, raising his hand to the door and pretending to unlock it, even though the spider was doing the job quite nicely by itself.

'Bye, Mrs Crab.'

Max slid round the door, then shut it

again quickly. There was a squeak and a loud thud from the other side. Max lifted the letter box and saw the caretaker squashed against the flat door like a bug on a car windscreen. Silently chuckling to himself, he

headed for the kitchen to see what had upset Fang.

Max pushed open the kitchen door and gasped at the mess inside. The table lay upside down in the corner of the room. Two chairs were on the cooker. The dustbin was wedged inside the washing machine and a mountain of food covered the floor; perched seesaw-like on the food mountain was a broken shelf.

'Fang,' called Max. 'Fang, where are you?'

'Help!'

Max spun round. He'd expected Fang to

bark, not talk. Was someone playing a joke?

'Fang, is that you?'

'Well, it's not Ned,' replied Fang smartly.

Max grinned. He'd looked after talking animals before, but it was still a surprise to hear an animal speak for the first time. Max picked his way through the mess until he saw a black nose peeping out from beneath a box of Witchos.

'What happened?' he asked, pulling the Witchos aside. 'Were you hungry?'

'Starving,' agreed Fang, wriggling free.

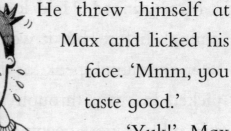 He threw himself at Max and licked his face. 'Mmm, you taste good.'

'Yuk!' Max pushed the puppy away. 'Go and lick something else.'

Fang stopped licking Max's face and started on his shoes.

'What happened here then?' asked Max.

'I don't know,' said Fang sheepishly. 'It was almost a full moon last night. I could see it through a chink in the curtain and it made me want to howl. Then I got hungry and went to get a snack. Only my biscuits are on the top shelf and I couldn't reach them. I was nibbling one of Ned's sticks to take my mind off my rumbly tummy when suddenly there was a bang and everything fell on top of me. I howled for help, but no one came.'

'No one knows you're here,' said Max. 'Ned's keeping you a secret because of the no-pets rule. No more howling. If you get found out, you'll have to leave.'

Fang's blue eyes grew as large as cauldrons.

'I don't want to leave. Ned's soooo nice!'

Max bent to pick up the chewed stick.

'Are you sure you're allowed to have this?'

'Yes,' said Fang, licking Max's nose. 'It's not Ned's best one. It's a spare. Mmmm, you taste scrummy.'

'Get off!' laughed Max.

The stick looked familiar, but it was so

badly chewed that Max couldn't
work out its function so he
propped it against the
washing machine.

'I'll clear up while
you're eating breakfast.
Then we'll go out.'

'Yippee!' squealed Fang.

Max slid his rucksack from his back and
dropped it on the floor.

'I brought sandwiches, drinks and a ball.
I thought we could go to the beach. I know
a nice one that's never busy.'

'Ooooh! Yes, yes, yes!' Fang ran round in
excited circles, almost knocking Max over.

'Calm down!' laughed Max.

Ned had left a huge supply of puppy
food. Max dished up a whole can of Meaty
Chunks, mixed it with a handful of dog

biscuits, then refilled Fang's water bowl with fresh water. He tidied up the kitchen while Fang ate.

'I'll put the broken shelf here,' he said, laying it on a worktop. 'Please don't break anything else. Ned won't be happy if he comes back to a wrecked flat.'

Fang grunted. He was busy pushing his bowl around in circles on the floor as he licked it clean.

'Yummy,' he sighed. 'That was delicious.'

The wicker basket to smuggle Fang from the building was next to a blackened cauldron. Under the silly frilly lid Max found a collar, an extending lead, a small plastic shovel for scooping up poo and a stack of plastic bags to put the poo in.

'Nice,' he said, pushing it up one end to make room. 'In you get.'

The moment Fang dived into the basket there was a loud crack. 'Whoops!' yelped Fang. 'Didn't see that there.'

'Fatty!' Max laughed, picking up the broken shovel. 'Luckily for me, it's the handle end that broke.'

Max pulled the cover back over the basket and pushed the stray tufts of Fang's grey fur out of sight.

'Ready?' he asked.

'Ready,' was the muffled reply.

'Don't make a sound. I don't even want to hear you breathing,' Max joked.

CHAPTER FOUR
WHERE IS MRS CRAB?

Max needed both hands to lift the basket. He staggered a few paces, then dumped it on the floor.

'Oomph!' he groaned. 'What a weight!'

'Must be those Meaty Chunks,' said Fang.

'It's this meaty chunk,' teased Max, pulling back the cover and poking Fang's round tummy. 'You're too heavy for me to carry you in this. How does Ned manage?'

'Ned doesn't use the basket. He says a funny rhyme that makes me invisible,' said Fang.

'Cool!' said Max. He'd guessed Ned was a wizard from some of the things he kept in his flat. That must be how he had got Fang out and then back inside the flats yesterday when they'd first met. He'd said the puppy was good at being invisible. Max realized that Ned hadn't been joking.

'Well, I can't do magic so I'll have to find another way of sneaking you outside.'

Max thought for a moment and then had a brainwave.

'You can ride in my rucksack. It's much lighter than the basket.'

It was a squeeze to fit Fang in the rucksack. Max left the zip partly open so he could breathe.

'Wheeee! This is FUN!' shouted Fang, as Max hoisted the bag on to his back.

'Shh!' whispered Max. 'We're leaving now.'

Max opened the door to the flat and cautiously headed for the stairs. He wished he'd remembered to tell Fang to keep still. Every now and then the puppy wriggled, which was a bit of a giveaway. But he needn't have worried. There was no sign of Mrs Crab in the reception hall, but there was a long line of people at the counter waiting to see her.

'She's never around when she's needed,' grumbled one.

'I spend half my days looking for her,' added another.

Nervously Max looked around. Where

had Mrs Crab gone after she'd followed him up to Ned's flat? Maybe she was hiding somewhere, waiting to catch him out? She had to be up to something, or she would be back in reception by now doing her job. Well, she wasn't going to catch Max out. He was a good pet sitter. No way was he going to let Mrs Crab find out about Fang. Ned had made it very clear what Mrs Crab would do to Fang if she caught him. She'd make him leave, or worse.

'Mrs Crab is evil,' Max muttered as he hurried to the door.

Safely outside, Max stood at the bottom of the stone steps while he decided on the quickest way to the beach.

'Pssst,' whispered Fang. 'You can let me out now.'

Max waited until he was almost at the

end of the drive before he stopped. The rucksack was heavy and he was glad to wriggle out of it and let Fang free. The moment Max unzipped his rucksack Fang leaped out and stretched his legs.

Suddenly a grey squirrel burst out from a bush.

'Yummy! A squirrel,' shouted Fang, tearing after it.

'Fang!' cried Max as the two animals raced back towards the flats.

Max chased after Fang, calling, 'Come back before someone sees you.'

Fang ignored him and chased the squirrel

into the back garden. Petals fell like confetti as the werepup hurtled through a large bed of autumn flowers. Max sprinted closer and dived for the puppy, but Fang wriggled free and Max was left clutching a tuft of grey fur.

Ned was right about Fang being a handful, thought Max.

Fang wasn't going to stay a secret for long if he carried on like this.

CHAPTER FIVE
ROCKET PAWS

Eventually Max caught up with the puppy at the base of a tree.

'Squirrel – one, Fang – zero, and serves you right,' he said, crossly.

'I only wanted to lick it,' said Fang forlornly. 'Squirrels taste yummy.'

Max pulled Fang's lead out of his rucksack and buckled the collar around his neck.

'Urrrrrrrggh!' yelled Fang. 'That's strangling me.'

Max slid a finger through the collar to check that it wasn't secured too tightly.

'It isn't!'

'It is!' said Fang crossly.

'Ned said I had to keep you a secret. Some secret! What if Mrs Crab had seen you?'

Fang hung his head.

'I'm sorry.'

'That's OK.'

'Will you take this off me now?'

'No way!'

'Not moving then,' said Fang, plonking his fat bottom down on the ground.

'Suit yourself,' said Max. 'We won't go to the beach.'

Max chuckled as Fang immediately leaped up, barking, 'Come on, slow toes.'

'Not so fast, rocket paws,' said Max, holding Fang back as he rushed towards the gate at the end of the garden.

The gate led to a bushy lane. At first Fang walked nicely by Max's side, but the werepup was too excited to stay there for long. Soon he was darting ahead or lagging behind to sniff at interesting smells. Each time Fang pulled in a different direction the extending lead got longer.

'It's like having a dog on a yo-yo,' Max laughed.

Luckily the beach wasn't far. The moment Fang's paws stepped on to the sand the werepup yelped with delight.

'Wait!'

Max almost had his arm pulled off as Fang galloped towards the farthest end of the beach before he stopped.

'That was great, wasn't it?' he panted.

'Yeah, great! If you like being tied to the end of a rocket,' agreed Max, spitting sand from his mouth.

He sat down and Fang jumped in his lap

to lick his face.

'Pooh! Get off! Your breath pongs!'

'So does yours,' said Fang cheerfully.

Max unclipped Fang's lead. He rummaged in his rucksack for a ball and threw it across the beach.

'Fang, fetch.'

'Fetch it yourself. You threw it,' said Fang.

Max looked at him suspiciously.

'It's a game. I throw a ball. You go and fetch it.'

'I'll do the throwing then,' said Fang.

'That's not how the game's played.'

'Then it's a stupid game,' said Fang. 'Let's dig a hole instead. We can both do that.'

Enthusiastically Fang began to dig, spraying sand everywhere.

'Fang, no! Stop it!' squeaked Max.

The puppy ignored him and carried on digging until Max grabbed him by the collar.

'You need training,' he said.

'Training?' Fang's blue eyes sparkled. 'I love trains.'

'Not trains! Training. Training is doing what you're told. So when I say sit, you sit. When I say down, you lie on the floor. And when I say fetch, you bring back the ball,' said Max.

'Sounds boring,' said Fang, lazily.

'It isn't. It's just what you need. We'll start now. It'll be fun. I promise.'

CHAPTER SIX
FULL MOON

Max spent all day with Fang. First he taught him the simple commands: sit, fetch and lie down. Then he took Fang for a walk along the beach to tire him out, in the hope that Fang wouldn't spend another night howling. It was such good fun that Max stayed out longer than he meant to. Dusk was falling when he and Fang finally arrived back at Seagull Towers. Under the cover of the trees at the bottom of the garden, Max took off his rucksack.

'In you get,' he said.

Fang shivered.

'I feel funny.'

'You are funny,' said Max. 'Hurry up and get in.'

'Look! The moon's out,' Fang stared up at the darkening sky. 'Ooh, it's huge! It must be . . .'

Suddenly Fang curled back his top lip and snarled.

'Wow! What big teeth you have,' joked Max.

'Grrrrrr!'

Fang began to tremble. 'What's happening to me?'

Tufts of longer fur were sprouting from his ears and paws. His claws grew longer and his eyes turned bluer.

'Grrrr!'

'Oh no!' groaned Max, suddenly remembering Ned's warning. 'It's a full moon. Quick! You've got to go indoors.'

'Nooooo,' howled Fang, throwing back his head and wailing loudly.

'Yes,' squeaked Max, trying to bundle Fang into his rucksack.

'Woooooo,' howled Fang, digging razor-sharp claws into the ground. 'Wooooooooo!'

Bravely Max shoved Fang into his rucksack, but the werepup was turning from a fat little puppy into a lean wolf cub and

329

fought back furiously.

'In you go,' shouted Max.

'Woooooo!' Fang yowled.

Fear gave Max extra strength. He grabbed Fang by the scruff of the neck and rammed his rucksack over the werepup's head. Fang had grown too big to fit inside, but Max held the bag in place shouting, 'Don't look at the moon!'

'Woooooo!' howled Fang, wriggling violently.

Max threw himself on the bag, pinning Fang to the ground. Fang kicked like an angry kangaroo, but Max held tight until gradually the werepup stopped struggling and fell silent. Was it his imagination or was Fang getting smaller again? Max continued to hold the puppy tightly, and after a very long while the puppy had shrunk enough to be squeezed back into the rucksack. Relieved, Max scooped the bag up in his arms and hurried towards the flats.

Max had almost reached the top of the stone steps when Fang launched a surprise attack, thrusting his head out of the top of the rucksack.

'Back!' shouted Max, struggling to push the puppy's head back in the bag.

'Wooooo!' howled Fang, gazing longingly at the moon.

Once again his top lip curled back, fur sprouted from his ears and paws, his claws grew longer and his eyes turned bright blue.

'Grrrrrrrrrrrrr,' he snarled, bursting from the rucksack just as Mrs Crab came through the revolving doors.

'A dog!' she shrieked. 'No dogs allowed. It's in the rules.'

She lunged at Fang, who darted sideways so that Mrs Crab almost fell down the stone steps.

'Sorry, Mrs Crab,' said Max politely. 'I found this puppy in the road. He's obviously a stray and I was taking him home when he escaped.'

'Get it out of here,' screeched Mrs Crab.

Fang snarled nastily and Mrs Crab turned scarlet with rage. Sticking out her enormous chest, she ran, tank-like, at him.

'Got you,' she shouted, grabbing him by the scruff of the neck. 'Ouch! Don't you try to bite me.' Mrs Crab gave Fang a hard shake as she dragged him back up the steps.

Max raced after her.

'Thanks, Mrs Crab. I'll take over now. The puppy's coming home with me.'

'I don't think so,' grunted Mrs Crab, squeezing Fang into the revolving doors. 'This is a DANGEROUS dog. First thing tomorrow I'm calling the vet to deal with it. We can't have dangerous animals running around. Now, out of my way before I have you dealt with too.'

CHAPTER SEVEN
THE ESCAPE

Max was in big trouble. There'd been a huge row at home for coming in late and his mum had sent him straight to his room after tea. Not that Max had eaten much. He was too worried about Fang. Mrs Crab had dragged Fang all the way to the boiler room, where she'd locked him inside.

Max had pleaded with her to let him take the puppy, but she'd refused and kept repeating, 'That dog is dangerous. The vet can deal with it tomorrow.'

Max hoped that Fang wouldn't feel too scared, shut up in the dark with a noisy old boiler. But Fang's comfort was the least of Max's problems. Max knew exactly what Mrs Crab had meant by getting the vet to 'deal' with Fang. She would have him put to sleep, like the dog that had chewed her favourite slippers.

'I've got to rescue Fang,' thought Max desperately.

Fang might be a bundle of mischief, but Max was already very fond of him. And what would Ned say if he knew the danger his pet was in? Miserably Max lay on his bed staring at the ceiling. Then, suddenly, he had an idea. Grinning, Max rolled over and reached for his alarm clock.

Very early the following morning Max arrived at Seagull Towers, leaned his bike against the stone staircase and tiptoed in through the revolving doors. The reception

hall was empty. Nervously Max glanced around before slipping behind Mrs Crab's counter. He went straight to her cabinet and rifled through the drawers. The first was jam-packed with paper clips, scissors, sticky tape and pens. The second contained a half-eaten pack of biscuits and a pile of new envelopes. But in the third Max got lucky. Right at the bottom, underneath an old newspaper, was a tin. Max opened it up and almost cheered with relief. Inside was a heap of keys, all neatly tagged and labelled.

'Boiler room,' said Max, triumphantly picking out the largest key.

He held the key tightly in his hand as he hurried across the reception hall and down the corridor to the boiler room. At first Max couldn't get the lock undone. Frustrated, he pulled the key back out and reread the label, but it was definitely the right key. Max pushed it back in slowly and jiggled it about. He was rewarded by a loud click, so he turned the handle and the door swung open.

'Woo, woo, woo,' yapped Fang, hurling himself at Max's legs as he quickly shut the door behind him. 'I'm sorry. What did I do? It must have been really bad for you to lock me up in here all night.'

Max stared at Fang in astonishment.

'Don't you remember?'

'No,' said Fang, shaking his head. 'Was I really naughty?'

'I didn't lock you up. It was Mrs Crab. You tried to bite her,' said Max.

'Nothing serious then,' said Fang, in relief.

'No, nothing serious,' replied Max.

'Except that now Mrs Crab wants to get rid of you.'

Fang wasn't listening. He had his nose inside an empty biscuit wrapper and was gobbling up the crumbs.

'I'm starving,' he said. 'I found some biscuits and guess what else I found? Come over here and I'll show you.'

'No,' said Max firmly. 'There isn't time. We've got to get out of here. This is serious. Mrs Crab is planning to have you put down.'

'Put down where?' asked Fang.

'Oh, never mind,' said Max. 'Quick, hop into my rucksack. I'm taking you out for the day so she can't find you.'

'Yippee!' squealed Fang.

He gave the biscuit wrapper one last lick, then scrambled inside Max's rucksack, but when Max turned the handle of the door it was stuck. He wiggled it and thumped it, but the door wouldn't budge. A trickle of sweat ran down Max's neck.

'Stay calm,' he told himself.

In the corner of the room Max saw a toolbox. He opened it, grabbed a hammer and gave the door handle a hard thump. There was an ominous crack, then the door swung open.

'Phew,' sighed Max, peering out into the corridor.

There was no one about. Max hared along to reception, replaced the boiler-room key, then hurried outside, almost bumping into Mrs Crab as she puffed up the stone steps.

'Good morning,' he said politely.

Mrs Crab smiled nastily.

'It will be when the vet arrives.'

'You're not ill, are you?' asked Max.

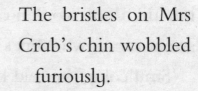

The bristles on Mrs Crab's chin wobbled furiously.

'The vet's not for me! It's for the dog that tried to savage me last night.'

'Oh,' said Max innocently. 'Of course.'

Max was keen to be as far away as possible when Mrs Crab found the boiler room empty. He unchained his bike and pedalled off as fast as he could, with Fang hidden in the rucksack, weighing heavily on his back. Max and Fang spent another great day on the beach, but this time Max was careful not to stay out too late. He sneaked Fang back into Seagull Towers long before dusk. Before he went home Max drew all of Ned's curtains so that not one chink of moonlight could shine into the flat. Then he made Fang promise to behave himself.

'I will,' said the puppy solemnly.

Before he left Max double-checked he'd locked Ned's door. He was hoping to leave unseen, but unfortunately Mrs Crab appeared in the corridor from the boiler room just as Max reached reception.

'You, boy!' she screeched, pointing a fat finger at him. 'Plant sitter indeed! Well, I'm watching you now. I know you've taken that dog. Don't think you're going to get away with it. I'll catch you out, and then you'll both be for it.'

She ran her finger across her throat,

leaving Max in no doubt as to what she meant.

'And I'm watching you too,' said Max under his breath.

There was something funny about Mrs Crab. She was never around when she was needed and always there when she wasn't. Max was sure she was up to something – if only he could find out what.

Chapter Eight
Flood

Arriving at Seagull Towers early the next morning, Max parked his bike, then bounced up the stone staircase. He spun through the revolving doors and found an elderly lady waiting in reception.

'Good morning,' she said. 'I'm looking for Mrs Crab. Have you seen her?'

'No, sorry,' said Max.

Cheerfully he hopped up the spiral staircase. If he was quick he could smuggle Fang out of the building before Mrs Crab appeared. But as Max entered the corridor leading to Ned's flat, he could see bubbles seeping under the door. Max's heart raced. What had Fang done now? Max pulled the spider key out of his pocket, urging it to hurry as it leaped into the lock. At last the front door opened and a wall of bubbles tipped into the corridor.

'Fang!' shouted Max, pushing through them. 'Urrrg, phwwt!'

The bubbles popped around him, filling his mouth with the taste of soap. His feet squelched on the slippery carpet. Carefully Max waded along the hall and opened the kitchen door. More bubbles spilled out. Max batted them aside calling, 'Fang, where are you?'

'Here, in the sink.'

Max couldn't see as far as the sink. He paddled through the kitchen, barging into the table as he headed towards Fang's voice.

'Fang?'

'Here.'

On the draining board, looking like a bubble sculpture, sat Fang. His ears were back and he was shaking.

'What happened?' asked Max.

Fang hung his head.

'I don't know.'

'You must know.'

'I don't.'

A funny gurgling sound made Max spin round. Not far from the sink was the washing machine, and millions of bubbles were spewing from its door. Max reached over and pressed the stop button, but the bubbles continued to churn from the machine.

'I tried that already,' said Fang miserably.

'How much soap powder did you use?' asked Max. 'One lorry full, or two?'

'I didn't' squeaked Fang. 'I never touched it.'

'As if!' said Max. 'Washing machines don't just switch themselves on.'

'It did,' wailed Fang. 'I was happily chewing this stick, keeping really quiet like you told me too, when there was a green flash and the bubbles started.'

'You're always only chewing on a stick,' said Max.

'I'll chew the furniture if you'd rather,' said Fang.

'Wait!'

Max picked up the stick and looked at it. There wasn't much left of the end, but he suddenly realized what it was.

'Oh, Fang!' Max couldn't help himself and burst out laughing. 'That's not a stick. It's a wand.'

'Yes!' Fang exclaimed. 'That's what Ned calls it! He does really clever things with it, even though it's only his spare.'

'What, like flooding the flat with bubbles?'

'No!' Fang's blue eyes widened. 'I didn't . . . did I?'

Max nodded.

Suddenly Fang was laughing too. He opened his mouth and howled.

'It's not funny,' giggled Max. He tried to look stern, but that made him laugh even more.

'Too right!' howled Fang. 'I nearly drowned. Can you make the bubbles go away?'

'I don't know.'

Max took some deep breaths and felt calmer. 'I could try stopping it with the wand, but it might not work now you've chewed the end.'

'Please try,' said Fang.

'Give it here then.'

'Fetch!' said Fang cheekily, throwing the wand to Max.

'Ha ha!' said Max, reaching out and catching the wand just as the kitchen door opened. He stared in horror.

'Er, hello, Mrs Crab. How did you get in?'

'The door was open,' snapped Mrs Crab. 'Why all the noise, and WHO made all this mess?'

'Me,' said Max. 'I'm doing some washing.'

'Washing?!' screeched Mrs Crab.

Her face was redder than a traffic light, and the bristles on her chin stuck out like daggers.

'NEVER, in forty years as caretaker, has anyone flooded one of my flats, until now.'

'It's Ned's flat, not yours!' growled Fang.

Mrs Crab spun round, confused. Max, finger to his lips, shook his head warningly at Fang. Fang's blue eyes widened. Then he quickly shut his mouth.

'Ha!' Luckily Mrs Crab was too angry to realize it was Fang who had spoken. 'I knew I'd catch you out in the end. It's that dangerous dog. I'm calling the vet to deal with it right now.'

Max wasn't sure what happened next. One moment he was holding Ned's wand in front of him, the next it was pointing straight at Mrs Crab's bristly chin. There was a loud crack, a strange hissing noise, then a stream of orange stars shot from the wand and whizzed around the kitchen. Max coughed. A lone star spluttered from the tip of the wand and fizzled away.

Behind him the washing machine belched loudly. Max spun round, punching the air with delight when he saw that it had finally turned itself off.

'I did it. I stopped the washing machine!' he cried, waving Ned's wand.

There was no reply. The kitchen was empty.

'Fang?' Max waded over to the sink, but Fang had gone. So had Mrs Crab, and a cold panic set in Max's stomach. Mrs Crab had taken Fang away. Something was thumping. It was louder than an army of marching giants. Max stared around the room before realizing that the noise was coming from his own heart. Suddenly he felt breathless, and that made him angry. How dare Mrs Crab take Fang away! He would follow her and demand she gave him back. As Max splashed to the door a voice called down the hall . . .

'Hello!'

CHAPTER NINE
MRS CRAB

'Is Mrs Crab here? I heard her voice.'

The elderly lady that had been waiting at Mrs Crab's desk in reception earlier stuck her head round the front door. Max was so relieved to see her that he laughed. For one awful moment he'd thought that Ned had come home early.

'What happened?' asked the lady kindly. 'Did the washing machine burst a pipe?'

'Several,' said Max, his brain whirring so fast he thought that it might burst too.

'Mrs Crab's gone. Didn't she pass you?'

'No, thank goodness.' The lady grinned.

'She's not the best person to meet in a narrow hallway.'

'Er, no. Quite,' said Max. 'Don't come any further. The floor's really slippery.'

Max stood in the kitchen doorway, blocking the lady's view. His heart was thumping again. He'd just noticed a large, rock-shaped creature half submerged in bubbles. It looked very out of place in Ned's kitchen. A horrible thought crossed Max's mind. No, that was ridiculous. It couldn't be, could it? Furtively Max glanced at the creature again and almost groaned out loud. This was turning into a nightmare! Max started to laugh. He always laughed when he was in trouble, even though this definitely wasn't a laughing matter.

'I need a bucket,' he said, forcing himself to be serious. 'Can you lend me one?'

'Of course I can!' said the lady. 'Back in a tick.'

Max didn't really need a bucket. He just needed the lady out of the way. When she'd gone Max shut the front door and put the chain across. Reluctantly he returned to the kitchen. The creature hadn't moved. Max bent down for a closer look at the large crab sitting on Ned's kitchen floor. It had six jointed legs, a pair of pincers, two beady black eyes and, unusually for a crab, bristles. Max prodded it with Ned's wand and the crab angrily waved a claw.

'Mrs Crab!' Max collapsed with laughter. 'Mrs Crab's turned into a crab! But how?'

'You did it.' Fang splashed through the kitchen door, and Max hugged him with relief.

'Where've you been? You gave me such a fright when you disappeared.'

'You said I was a secret so I hid.'

'Oh, Fang!' Max hugged the werepup again. 'It's too late. Mrs Crab saw you.'

'I know. So you turned her into a crab,' said Fang, chuckling.

'I didn't mean to!' Guiltily, Max stared at the wand. 'Oh bat poo!'

'But that's good! Now she can't send for the vet. Thank you, Max. You're the best pet sitter ever.'

Fang threw himself on Max, causing

a mini tidal wave that sent the crab scuttling away.

'Quick,' said Max, splashing after her. 'Shut the door before she escapes.'

Fang nosed the door shut.

'We'll have to put her somewhere safe. I know! The bath,' said Max.

He put Ned's wand on the table, but as he drew closer to Mrs Crab she snapped her enormous claws at him.

'Pinch me and I'll put you on the barbecue,' Max threatened.

Mrs Crab's shell turned scarlet. She banged a claw on the ground, splattering Max with bubbles, but she didn't pinch him when he lifted her up. She weighed a ton, and Max crossed the kitchen groaning,

'Out of the way, Fang.'

Max knew nothing about crabs, apart

from the fact that they were sea creatures. He went to the bathroom, put a few centimetres of cold water into the bath and threw in Ned's toy duck for company.

Then, shutting the bathroom door firmly behind him, he went to answer a knock at the front door.

It was the lady with two buckets and a sponge.

'Thanks,' said Max.

'Need any help?' she asked.

'No, thanks.'

'Well, if you're sure.' The lady sounded disappointed. 'If you change your mind, I'm in number sixteen.'

'Thanks,' said Max. 'And thanks for the buckets.'

When the lady had gone Max bolted the front door. Fang was sitting on the kitchen table chewing Ned's wand. Max snatched it away.

'Don't chew that!' he scolded.

'I'm a puppy. It's my job to chew things,' said Fang.

'I'm the pet sitter. It's my job to stop you,' said Max, examining the wand. The end was soggy and badly chewed. Experimentally Max waved it about. Did he dare use it to turn Mrs Crab back into herself? Perhaps he should try using it for something else first. Max decided to have a go at clearing up the kitchen.

'Stand back,' he told Fang.

Nervously Max waved the wand over a small patch of floor.

'Wand, dry. Please.'

A flash of red light burst from the wand, instantly melting the bubbles. A spiral of steam curled upwards as the floor dried.

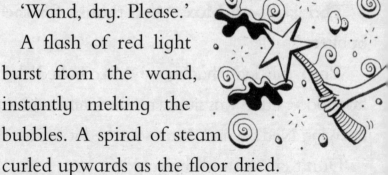

'Go, Max!' cheered Fang.

'Wicked!' exclaimed Max, and feeling braver he waved the wand around again.

'Wand, dry. Please,' he repeated.

Another flash of red. Hiss, pop, crack. The bubbles burst, sounding like a giant bowl of Rice Krispies. Steam rose from the floor and soon the kitchen was hotter than a jungle.

'Phew!' said Max, opening the window. 'That didn't take long.'

With the kitchen dry, Max started on the hall. 'Wand, dry,' he said more boldly this time.

There was a flash of red, lots of steam and a bitter smell.

'Poo!' said Max, then, realizing he'd set fire to the carpet, he waved the wand again.

'Wand, fire out.'

The flames spluttered and went out, leaving a small charred patch.

'Wicked!' sighed Fang. 'Shame about the carpet though.'

'Silly me!' agreed Max. 'Cos you'd never make a mess, would you?!'

CHAPTER TEN
FANG RUNS OFF

Max was in a dilemma. Deep down he knew he must use Ned's wand to turn Mrs Crab back into her human self. Crabby as she was (Max sniggered at the bad joke), it wasn't right to leave her in that state. But Fang was dead against the idea.

'Don't do it,' he wailed dramatically. 'She's going to have me dealt with, and what then? Ned would never forgive you.'

'But I can't leave her as she is,' said Max. 'What if she's got a family who'll miss her? We'll just have to be more careful. Especially you! No more howling and no more chewing Ned's wand.'

Before Max changed Mrs Crab back he made Fang hide in Ned's bedroom wardrobe.

'What if she comes looking for me?' he asked.

'She won't,' said Max firmly. 'I'll have Ned's wand, remember. If she tries anything funny, I'll turn her back into a crab.'

'Wicked,' said Fang. 'I hope she does.'

'Shh,' said Max as he closed the wardrobe door.

Slowly he went into the bathroom.

'Ugh!' he exclaimed. 'She must be hungry!'

Mrs Crab was eating Ned's duck; only its plastic beak remained. Experimentally Max waved the wand, then, pointing it at the bath, he said clearly, 'Wand, undo.'

There was a loud crack. Black smoke shot from the end of the wand, smothering everything. Max held his breath, wondering if his spell had worked. Then suddenly the air cleared and Max bit his tongue, trying not to laugh. There, in a bath of cold water, sat Mrs Crab. Her clothes were soaking and she had a plastic duck's beak stuck on her nose.

Max passed her one of Ned's towels, saying, 'Hello, Mrs Crab. Did you enjoy your bath?'

Mrs Crab pulled the duck beak from her nose. She shook her head a few times, then slowly stood up. Water gushed from her clothes like a waterfall.

'I'm not sure how I got here, but this I do know,' she growled. 'I'm going to catch that dog if it's the last thing I do.'

Mrs Crab climbed out of the bath and marched out of the bathroom.

Max guessed that Mrs Crab wouldn't go back to work straight away and he was right. There was no sign of her when he smuggled Fang out of the building for their daily outing. All this sneaking in and out was beginning to get to Max, and he wished there was some way of making Mrs

Crab leave him and Fang alone. After a fun day out on the beach, Max was starving and looking forward to going home for his tea. He let Fang walk to the top of Seagull Tower's drive before stopping to hide him in his rucksack.

'In you go, fatty,' he teased.

Fang stood stiller than a statue. Then suddenly he took off towards the flats.

'Fang,' shouted Max. 'Fang, come back. I was only joking.'

Fang ignored him. He raced up the stone steps and through the revolving doors. Max followed, accidentally whirling round twice before he managed to jump out. He was in time to see Fang speed off down the corridor towards the boiler room.

'Fang,' hissed Max, half cross, half scared. What was the werepup up to? He was behaving as if he wanted to get caught. When Max finally caught up with Fang he was throwing himself at the boiler-room door. Max grabbed him by the collar and hauled him backwards. Fang stuck his claws in the carpet and refused to move.

'Someone's in there,' he yapped. 'Can't you hear them shouting for help?'

Max stared at Fang suspiciously, but the werepup was serious. Then he heard it too. Inside the boiler room someone was wailing like a baby.

'I wonder who Mrs Crab's locked in there this time,' said Max angrily. 'Hello?' He banged on the door with his fist. 'Are you all right?'

There was no reply, but when Max pressed his ear to the door he heard a groan. Then he noticed the key was in the lock.

He turned it, but nothing happened. Then he wiggled the key this way and that, but the lock was jammed. He tried to force the door open. He banged and banged but it wouldn't budge.

'Shall I get Ned's wand?' offered Fang.

'No need.'

Suddenly, remembering a police raid in a film he'd watched, Max aimed a karate-style kick at the door lock. The door shuddered. Max kicked out again, and this time the lock broke and the door flew open.

'Wow!' said Fang, staring at the damage. 'How wicked was that?'

'As wicked as a hippo on ice skates,' said Max. 'But not as careful!'

CHAPTER ELEVEN
THE DEAL

Lying on the boiler-room floor, with a folding chair wedged on top of her, was Mrs Crab. She looked so funny that Max had a job not to laugh out loud. She was moaning, but she wasn't hurt and recovered

immediately when Max helped her up.

'The door lock's bust,' she grumbled. 'I couldn't get out. I was trying to unscrew the door hinges when I fell off the chair. I shouted for help but nobody came. I've been stuck in here all day.'

'That happened to me!' said Fang.

Max glared at him, wishing Fang had had the sense to hide, but it was too late. Mrs Crab spun round. Her eyes narrowed.

'It's that dog!' she exclaimed. She was too excited at having caught Max out to realize that it was Fang who'd spoken. 'And this time I'm calling for the vet.'

Mrs Crab pushed her way past Max.

'Wait,' he called. 'It was Fang who heard you shouting. He led me to you.'

'And?' said Mrs Crab nastily.

'And . . .'

Suddenly Max noticed an untidy pile of newspapers next to the boiler. He stepped closer and pulled them aside. Underneath was a kettle, a mug, a jar of coffee and several packets of biscuits.

'That's why no one can ever find you! You've been skiving off work, hiding in here drinking coffee and stuffing yourself with biscuits.'

The bristles on Mrs Crab's chin trembled and Max could see she was scared.

'You have, haven't you?' He grinned. 'Well, here's the deal: if you promise not to phone the vet and you let Fang stay here at Seagull Towers, then I won't tell anyone that you've been skiving. After all, you wouldn't want to lose your job, would you?'

For once, Mrs Crab was speechless.

★

The following day, Max and Fang sat on the steps that led up to Seagull Towers waiting for Ned to come home.

'Ooooh!' squealed Fang.

'What?' asked Max. 'Can you see Ned?'

'No.' Fang dived into the bushes. 'I need to go.'

'Again? You've only just been.'

'I can't help it,' said Fang, his black nose just visible through the branches. 'I always go when I'm excited.'

'Hurry up,' said Max. 'Ned's coming up the drive right now.'

'Oooooh!' Fang ran back and nearly knocked Max over.

'Whoa!' Max grabbed him by the collar. 'Slow down. You can't go to meet Ned like that. He'll think you're a mobile tree.'

Hurriedly Max picked leaves and twigs from Fang's coat. The werepup strained on the collar, growling like an engine. When Max finally let him go he raced towards Ned, who was staggering up the drive with two suitcases and a long package.

'Hello, hello, hello,' Fang barked. 'I've missed you soooooo much.'

'And I've missed you too,' said Ned, dumping the bags and scooping Fang up in his arms. 'Have you been good, or were you a wicked little werepup?'

'Fang's been very good,' said Max. 'We went for walks, we played on the beach and –' Max winked at Fang – 'we even did some crabbing.'

'Nothing exciting then,' said Ned cheerfully. 'Never mind, Daddy's home now and spider's teeth is he going to liven this place up! Down with silly rules! Look what my sister gave me as a thank-you for helping her out with the youth club.'

Ned pulled the paper away from the mysterious long package to reveal a shiny new skateboard.

'Wicked!' said Fang. 'Can I have a go?

'Visitors first,' said Ned, holding it out to Max.

'Thanks,' said Max, longing to try the skateboard but thinking he'd broken enough rules already, 'but I can't stop. I've got another pet to look after now. Take care, Fang! You too, Ned!'

Me and Fang!

ABOUT THE AUTHOR

Julie Sykes is an award-winning author
of over fifty books, mostly about animals
and magic. She lives with her family and
their wolf in a cottage in Hampshire.
When Julie isn't busy writing, she spends
her time eating cake, reading, sailing
and walking. You can visit Julie at
www.juliesykes.co.uk

ABOUT THE ILLUSTRATOR

Nathan Reed graduated from
Falmouth College of Art in 2000.
He has illustrated children's books for
Puffin and HarperCollins as well as
for Macmillan and Campbell Books.
Nathan lives in London.